D0031200

DOCTOR DOLITTLE'S
PUDDLEBY ADVENTURES

OTHER BOOKS BY HUGH LOFTING

DOCTOR DOLITTLE AND THE GREEN CANARY

DOCTOR DOLITTLE AND THE SECRET LAKE

DOCTOR DOLITTLE'S RETURN

DOCTOR DOLITTLE IN THE MOON

DOCTOR DOLITTLE'S GARDEN

DOCTOR DOLITTLE'S CARAVAN

DOCTOR DOLITTLE'S ZOO

DOCTOR DOLITTLE'S CIRCUS

DOCTOR DOLITTLE'S POST OFFICE

THE VOYAGES OF DOCTOR DOLITTLE

THE STORY OF DOCTOR DOLITTLE

Weekly Reader Childrens Book Club
presents

Especially Selected and Edited by
Weekly Reader Book Club

Library of Congress Catalog Card Number: 52-7457

Weekly Reader Book Club Edition
Intermediate Division

Contents

THE GREEN BREASTED MARTINS

THE LOST BOY

DOCTOR DOLITTLE'S
PUDDLEBY ADVENTURES

Introduction

DOCTOR DOLITTLE AND HIS FAMILY

IN THE BEGINNING Doctor Dolittle was a people's doctor. He prescribed pills and tonics and mended broken bones the way regular doctors do. Besides working at the profession of doctoring sick people he also doctored animals. In the course of caring for his animal friends he acquired so many regular animal boarders in his house that there was barely room for a human patient to get in the front door. He had white mice in the piano, rabbits in the pantry, and a pig who slept in the vegetable bin. Even the linen closet was occupied by a family of squirrels.

When his human patients complained of the crowding and refused to come to him unless he got rid of the animals, Doctor Dolittle stopped doctoring humans entirely; he became an animal doctor only. Polynesia, the parrot who became a member of the Doctor's household, helped him change from a people's doctor to an animal doctor. She taught him to speak the language of the animals. Being a parrot, Polynesia could talk in two languages—people's language and animal language. She was able to explain to the Doctor the meanings of the nose-twitching, ear-scratching and tail-wagging signals that make up the language of animals.

"But, Polynesia," said John Dolittle, "birds don't have noses to twitch and ears to wag and—a—er—it's all too confusing."

"Not at all, Doctor," replied Polynesia. "Birds speak a language all their own. Just listen to those nut hatches on the window-ledge. Hear how they chatter and whistle and make clucking noises. The little fellow—the one with the dark markings on his wings—he's showing his friend the sights around Puddleby. He just told the other one that this is Doctor Dolittle's house."

"My goodness! You don't say so!" said John Dolittle. "Do let me write it down." He rushed to his desk and brought out a notebook. "Now tell it slowly," he said as he scribbled away. "I must get it all down so that I won't forget."

It wasn't long before Doctor Dolittle was able not only to understand what the animals were saying but to speak their language as well. At first it was difficult because he had to learn to twitch his nose and scratch his ears as they did. The hardest part was the tail; he had to use his coat tails for that. The animals were amazed at the strange way the Doctor's coat tails flew around when he spoke to them. But very soon they became accustomed to it and understood him as well as they did their own animal friends.

Dab-Dab, the duck, was the Doctor's housekeeper. She cooked and scrubbed, dusted and cleaned, and went to market twice a week to keep the larder filled with assorted foods for the Doctor's strange family.

Gub-Gub, the pig, who also lived with the doctor, fancied himself an authority on foods. He had a great curiousity that was always getting him into trouble.

The household accounts and the Doctor's business dealings were taken care of by Too-Too, the owl, who was a famous mathematician—among animals, of course.

Jip, the dog, had many duties. He organized and helped build and manage the Home for Crossbred Dogs which occupied a large part of the Doctor's garden. Whenever there was a job of scenting to be done, Jip had no equal. He could follow the trail of a man who was miles away simply by identifying the tobacco the man smoked.

When small objects—some as small as a pin—had to be found, Whitey, the white mouse went to work. He had microscopic eyes and could see even the colours of a grain of dust.

Another member of the family was Chee-Chee, the monkey, who spent part of the time with the Doctor at Puddleby-on-the-Marsh and the other part in Africa where the climate was more to his liking. Whenever the Doctor went on a voyage he always sent for Chee-Chee to act as guide in following hidden trails and paths through jungles and foreign lands. He would climb the highest trees and swing along from limb to limb through the tangle of branches, calling out to the Doctor and his party the way the paths led.

Among the Doctor's animal friends who lived at Puddleby a good deal of the time, was a two-headed animal called a pushmi-pullyu. He had a head at each end of his body and could eat with one while talking with the other. The pushmi-pullyu said this enabled him to avoid talking with his mouth full.

Cheapside, the London sparrow who made his home in the ear of a statue on St. Paul's Cathedral in London where he could see everything and know everyone who passed through the great city, was perhaps the most versatile of the Doctor's friends. John Dolittle often called on him for information about the movements of ships and people, and Cheapside never failed to find the answers.

Early in his career as an animal doctor, John Dolittle took into his home a young boy by the name of Tommy Stubbins. Tommy, as the Doctor's chief assistant, learned to speak the language of animals and helped Doctor Dolittle with their care. Because the Doctor was a busy man it was Tommy Stubbins who wrote down the adventures of the great doctor and his animal friends.

In the little town of Puddleby-on-the-Marsh, where the Doctor and his family lived, Matthew Mugg, the Cat's-Meat-Man, sold food for animals. Naturally he came to be a great friend of the Doctor and Tommy and often assisted them in their problems with the animals.

There were others who lived with the Doctor for short periods: Kling, the Dog Detective, Dapple, the prize Dalmatian, Toby and Swizzle, the circus dogs, and Bumpo, the African Prince—son of the king of Jolliginki.

The stories which follow in this book were written by Tommy Stubbins about the Doctor and his animal friends.

Olga Michael

Dapple

CHAPTER ONE

THE CHAMPION

I THINK that of all of my experiences as manager of the Dolittle Zoo I enjoyed those connected with the Home for Crossbred Dogs the most. Of course I had always known that there was a great variety in the characters and personalities of dogs; but I certainly never realized *how* great a variety till I began to take part in the daily life of this mongrels' club.

There was one member of the Home who was thoroughbred. This was Dapple the Dalmatian. Not only was he thoroughbred, he was a prizewinner with a pedigree ever so long and gold medals and ribbons and honourable mentions to his credit from nearly all the big dog shows. For these reasons he was not, strictly speaking, eligible as a member of the Home. And when he first arrived there were certain members who objected because he wasn't a mongrel. But Dapple explained to the committee that it wasn't after all his fault that he was born thoroughbred, and as he was already very popular with almost every dog in the club, he was finally accepted in spite of his aristocratic breeding.

He was one of those dogs whose coming to the Dolittle Zoo had caused the Doctor a good deal of trouble with their owners. Dapple belonged to a most extraordinary lady. She was very stout and used to make herself look still larger by the ruffles and frills she wore. Jip always said that she reminded him of an enormous, highly-scented cream puff.

. . . an enormous cream puff

When Dapple first ran away to join the club she came after him (in a carriage and pair with two footmen) and took him away again. She blamed the Doctor for his coming. But Dapple ran away so many times that finally she saw it was no use. It was clear that the dog himself preferred the simple joys of the mongrels' club to the extravagant luxury of her elaborate household. So, saying that the dog couldn't after all really be thoroughbred to desert *her* home for a mere zoo, she turned up her nose and bade her pet good-bye for the last time—to Dapple's great delight—and departed.

I don't just know how it came about, but this dog was selected to tell the first of some after-dinner stories (or autobiographies, as I called them in my book). And when John Dolittle and I came into the dining room one evening, we found Dapple already installed on the speaker's platform and the rest of the club sitting around waiting. The committee did not want the story to begin till the Doctor and I should arrive.

Our appearance was welcomed with yelps of greeting and sighs of relief. I found myself a comfortable corner where I could spread out my papers for taking down the record. The Doctor was at once surrounded and carried off to another corner by all his adoring friends, who wanted to sit beside him. Silence gradually settled down over the dining room and Dapple began.

"I fancy," Dapple said, "that my story's chief interest for you will lie in the fact that it is the story of a thoroughbred's life. How often have I envied you happy mongrels! For my existence from the beginning was a monotonously thoroughbred existence. With my entrance into your club this week, I have, almost for the first time, obtained that liberty which you have enojoyed all your days.

"I will begin from the time when I and two of my brothers and two sisters found ourselves in a dog shop on sale. We were put into a little pen with straw on the bottom and 'PEDIGREED PUPPIES' written across the front. To begin with we didn't like it at all. But you know the way puppies are: it didn't take us long to forget our troubles and we soon began to play and wrestle together and had a pretty good time. The boy who looked after us and gave us our meals was a very nice lad; and whenever he wasn't busy he would join in our games.

"Customers would come into the shop and look at us. And one by one my brothers and sisters were all sold and I was the last to be left. I felt very sad about this at first. But the shop-boy did his best to console me and took me out for walks after his work was done.

" 'Dapple,' he used to say, 'you're the best looking pup of the whole family. Those customers don't know anything about dogs—for all their knowing airs they put on—or they would never have left you to the last. But I'm glad they have. I wish I had the money to buy you myself. But you're so expensive. That's on account of your pedigree, you see. Five pounds. Think of it! For a little round dumpling like you! You should feel proud. And me only earning five shillings a week!'

"I used to watch the customers that came in. I grew to like the shop-boy more and more. And as time went on I became less and less anxious to be sold. I used to pretend to be very ill-natured so the customers wouldn't buy me. When they'd put their hands into the pen to stroke me I'd growl and show my teeth.

" 'Oh!' they'd say. 'Snappish, eh? No, I don't want that dog. Couldn't trust him with the children.'

"And to my great relief they'd leave my cage and go on to look at the collie pups who lived next door to me. But one day a man came in whose cheerful smiling face I rather liked from the very beginning. As usual I growled to show that I wasn't to be trusted with children, as soon as he tried to pet me. But, to my great surprise, he took not the slightest notice. Maybe he didn't have any children. Anyway he seemed to know that I was just putting it all on, because instead of

"I started to play"

starting back and going away, he just laughed and went right on stroking me. And soon I gave up trying to scare him off and started to play. He seemed such a jolly, honest, nice man that I didn't mind even if he did buy me.

"Well, in the end the man bought me and took me away

to his country home. It was a very nice home and I felt sure right from the start that I had been very lucky and was going to enjoy my life there. My owner seemed to be a sort of country gentleman—not terribly rich, but quite well off. He didn't work. His time was occupied fishing and hunting and looking after his very large and lovely country estate.

"It appeared that the shop-boy had been right and that I was destined to turn out a very specially fine specimen of the Dalmatian breed. As soon as I began to grow up a little all of my owner's friends who came to stay with him made flattering remarks about me and prophesied that I was surely going to be a prizewinner. In time my owner began entering me for dog shows. Oh, dear, how I hated those shows! For weeks beforehand I used to get dieted and scrubbed and brushed and trimmed and fixed so I would look my very best. I wasn't allowed to go out in muddy weather lest I mess up my immaculate coat or get my nails dirty. And when the show came off I had to sit for hours on a bench waiting for the silly judges to come around and examine me—when all I wanted was to be out in the nice wet fields chasing hares or digging for rats.

"I took many prizes—ever so many. I suppose, as such things go, I really had a wonderful career. For three years I carried off the highest honors in the Dalmatian class from every show I was entered for. My picture was in all the sporting papers. And I even had my portrait painted in oil colours by a famous artist. I got a stiff neck standing still while it was being done.

"But I didn't care for my show career a bit. My owner seemed to realize this and as soon as the shows were over he would always let me out in the fields to get as dirty as I liked and have a good time till the next show came along. It amused him. He even used to get dirty himself, helping me to dig for rats.

"This very nice man was fond of betting on the race horses. This was his ruin. He was just as unsuccessful on the racetrack as he was successful at the dog shows. He lost and lost and lost. Soon he began to have to sell things to make good his losses. Part of his fine country estate was put on the market. Then some of his horses, beauties, they were. One thing after another went, but still he wouldn't stop betting. He was always hoping that he'd make a big win and get back all he had lost.

"I began to wonder when I would get sold. I knew that at the shows he had been offered tremendous sums for me by millionaire dog fanciers. And much as he liked me—we were tremendous friends—it would only be natural, with all this need for money pressing on him, that some day he'd be tempted to part with me.

"After a few more months things got so bad that my owner was actually in want. There were many days when he didn't get enough to eat. And I created quite a sensation by bringing him home chickens which I took from the poulterer's shop in the village as I passed. It never occurred to me, I'm afraid, that there was anything wrong in my taking them. But the poulterer seemed to think there was. And I realized, after I had been caught and taken to the police station a second time, that I was giving my owner a good deal more trouble than profit.

"Of course as things went from bad to worse it began to look quite unavoidable that I must be sold. For even some of his household servants had not been paid their wages in a very long time.

"The day came. A woman who had often admired me at

the shows offered a particularly high price when the poor man was at his wits' end for money. He made the farewell short—for which I was glad. Neither of us cared for emo-

". . . bringing home chickens from the poulterer's shop as I passed"

tion or a show of sentiment, and if I had to go I wanted to do so quickly and as quietly as possible.

" 'I'm sorry, Dap,' said he giving me a final pat on the head. 'I feel horribly guilty, selling you. But—well, good-bye and good luck to you, old boy.'

"I felt dreadfully sad—and resentful, too. Not against him, for I saw that as the situation was it couldn't be helped now, but against my pedigree. If I hadn't been so beastly well bred my value would have been only a few shillings. And it would have hardly been worth any one's while to sell me.

"As I was led away by my new fat mistress I muttered to myself, 'Oh, why, *why* wasn't I born a mongrel?'

"Then my life entered upon an entirely new chapter. The woman who bought me was fabulously rich. She had enough servants and carriages and silver dishes and porcelain bath-tubs for six people. I shall never forget my disgust the first evening when I was brought to her home. Tea was being served and her drawing room was full of women guests, all jabbering and munching cakes. She had me led in to show me off to them.

" 'My dears,' she cackled, 'isn't he a beauty? I paid a terrible price for him. But I just *had* to have him—to go with my new gown, you know. The spots on his coat match the polka-dot silk perfectly—just perfectly!' "

CHAPTER TWO

A WILD BREAKFAST PARTY

"Can you imagine my disgust?"

Dapple's elegant, well-bred nose seemed to curl upward with scorn as he appealed to his audience. He was surely a beautiful creature to look at. Dalmatians were a more popular breed then than they are now. As a boy I had always called them "plum-pudding dogs," on account of their black spots. But I don't know that I had ever seen a thoroughbred champion before. And certainly such a homely title did not seem at all fitting for as fine a dog as this.

"That was what I had come to," he went on. "That was all my wellbredness and pedigree were to mean in the end: to be bought by an hysterical, cackling, empty-headed woman *because I matched her new polka-dot gown!* The shame of it—for a sporting dog like me! I was now to be part of a boudoir's furnishings. I ground my teeth with rage. And that very night of my arrival was the first time I ran away—the first time out of a dozen.

" 'So I'm to match a polka-dot dress, am I?' I muttered furiously. 'All right. Then I'll get rid of my spots.'

"I knew John Dolittle well, of course, and I came straight to his home as soon as I got away.

" 'Doctor,' I said, 'I want you to paint out my spots, or dye me a new colour, or something. I just will not be part of that woman's wardrobe. She wants to take me out on a string so people will stare at us and say how smart she is. You must do something. I simply can't bear the thought—the fat nincompoop!'

"Well, the Doctor sympathized with me and I do believe

"Then she put some perfume on me"

he might have done it if he hadn't had so many rows already about dogs running off from their owners to come and join his club in the Zoo here. I hung around still trying to persuade him, and while I was at it the wretched woman herself turned up to claim me. She had had me traced by droves of detectives. She is so horribly rich.

"So back I had to go to my doom as a boudoir ornament She hugged me and kissed me with joy at getting me back Then she put some perfume on me. She said I ought to use the same perfume as she wore. Think of it: me—*perfumed.*

"Oh, I forgot to mention that this woman had a husband It isn't any wonder that I forgot to mention him, because he really wasn't of any account anyway. He was just a husband to her—and a nuisance to me. He used to get bossed and hen-pecked to death by his wife and I suppose he felt *he* had to boss some one, so he tried to boss me. She used to send him to take me out for runs in the evening and he was always try-ing to teach me silly tricks which I didn't want to know, shouting orders at me in a loud voice so the passers-by could see what a masterful character he was. He would send me on errands to fetch his walking-stick, which he would de-liberately leave behind against a tree or a wall. So silly! I usually brought back a dead rat, if I could find one, or a ba-nana skin instead. I already knew a whole lot of good tricks. But the only fun I got out of these was trying to spoil his show and appearing as stupid as I could possibly be. Then he used to make me carry his newspaper in my mouth, but I always dropped it in the first puddle I passed.

"What a life! And how I longed to get away from it! One of the most terrible things about it was that I began to find my own character changing. My old owner had been a healthy, outdoor man of a calm, sensible disposition. With him I had grown into a sensible, sporting country dog. Now, being constantly with this hysterical woman who was always weeping over me—she insisted on telling me all her troubles, which were wholly imaginary and quite tiresome—I found to my horror that I was becoming a snappy, irritable, spoiled lap-dog. Like her, in fact. It was a dreadful discovery. I was always running away, but I always got brought back again.

"I practised in front of one of the mirrors"

My one ambition was to get into the Doctor's club here and become once more a calm, sensible, worth-while dog. Then I thought that maybe I'd have better luck if I went back to my old owner next time I escaped. I hoped, somehow, he'd keep me. Well, I got to his place after a long and strenuous journey only to find that his home had now been sold to someone else and he had gone abroad.

"Then, after I had been brought back to the scented boudoir for about the tenth time, I thought up a new plan. I had seen a mad dog on the streets one day and noticed that every one was in great terror lest he bite someone. His eyes flashed and his mouth frothed. I practised in front of one of the boudoir mirrors, making my eyes flash—terrible. Then I stole a piece of shaving soap from the husband's dressing room and practised making my mouth foam with lather. It wasn't pleasant but it looked wonderful.

" 'Good!' I said to myself as I went to bed that night after my secret rehearsal. 'To-morrow I'll be a mad dog. Then they'll *have* to get rid of me.'

"I have done a few crazy things in my life," the Dalmatian continued, "but never, I think, anything quite so crazy as pretending I was a real crazy dog. It is a wonder I'm alive. You see, with the case I had seen on the streets—when the mad dog went running round with staring eyes and frothing mouth —things happened differently. The people just fled away from him, scared blue. I didn't know that it is the custom to shoot mad dogs. I suppose nobody had a gun handy that time. But this time they had—several.

"Well, to begin from the beginning: I had timed my outbreak of madness to take place while my mistress was having breakfast. I had kept my piece of shaving soap handy from the night before, and while she was drinking her first cup of coffee I got it all frothy in my mouth. It was her habit to give me a lamb cutlet at breakfast time. She had no idea of feeding dogs. I was already losing my figure from being continually fed between meals. That's how she lost her figure too—

if she ever had one—by eating tit-bits at odd times. So my lamb cutlet, specially cooked, was brought in by the footman on a silver tray in the usual manner, and my mistress took it

"The footman jumped through the window"

by the paper frill and called to me:

" 'Come along, Dappy darling,' said she. 'Mama give little Dapsy his breakfast.'

"That's the way she used to talk. It almost spoiled my

appetite many a time. I came up to her, but instead of taking the cutlet, I took her hand in my teeth—not to bite her, really, you understand. Poor old thing, she certainly meant to be kind enough. But I had to play the part of a mad dog properly. She started back with a scream. Then I snarled and big gobs of white soapsuds slobbered from my mouth. I rolled my eyes. Then I threw a sommersault and bit the carpet. Next I bit the footman in the leg—I owed him one anyway. Then I bit the table in the leg and the breakfast dishes capsized with a crash onto the floor. After that I leapt on to the sofa and let out a bloodcurdling howl like a lost wolf.

"My mistress sprang up and ran for the door. The footman had already jumped through the window—into a bed of geraniums.

" 'Oswald!' the woman shrieked—that was her husband's name—'Oswald! Come quick! The dog's gone mad!' "

CHAPTER THREE

MAD DOG!

"Well, Oswald came. But he didn't stay very long. I made one snarling rush at him and he, too, dived through the window into the geraniums.

"Then the butler arrived on the run. Bells were ringing, doors slamming and people yelling all over the house by this time. The butler was a fat and pompous booby. He was armed with a golf club. I tore his pants for him as soon as he appeared, and all he succeeded in doing with the golf club was to smash a couple of valuable vases on the mantelpiece. He, too, beat a hasty retreat—to get more help, he said. Meantime I rushed round the breakfast room in circles, tossing cushions in the air, tearing down the curtains, upsetting furniture, howling, blowing soap bubbles all over the place. Oh, I was the grandest thing in mad dogs you ever saw.

"The trouble was I was too good. After I had thoroughly wrecked the breakfast room I dashed out into the hall, pulling down a hatrack playfully as I passed, and from there I rushed on into the garden. In the garden, for the first time, I realized what I had done. All over the place, behind bushes and trees and things, I saw men lurking with guns. *Bang! Bang! . . . Bang! Bang!* I was fired on from all sides. The noise was like a war. How I escaped goodness only knows. She had about twenty gardeners, but I suppose that they were all, luckily, bad shots. They didn't hit me. The only one that got hit was the butler—in the pants, the same pants that I had already torn. He got over it all right. But, poor man, it was his unlucky day.

"I sped right down to the end of the garden, making for a gate whose bars I knew I could get through. I reached it in safety, gained the road and raced away in the direction of the Doctor's house. Behind, the yells and shots of the enemy followed hot on my heels.

" 'Mad dog!' they bawled. 'Look out! His bite's poisonous! Shoot him! Mad dog!'

"Every one ahead of me ran for their gates, climbed lampposts, popped behind doors, leapt over walls, anything to get away from poor me, the enemy of society. It began to look as though I had been a bit too clever and that my grand plan might cost me my life.

" 'The Doctor,' I kept muttering to myself as I stretched out at full speed. 'He's my one chance. He can explain to these idiots. The Doctor! I'll be all right if I can only reach

"Behind bushes men were lurking with guns"

John Dolittle's house before they fill my hide full of lead.'

"As I raced down the road I began to wonder not only whether I was really crazy myself, but also whether the whole world had gone crazy, too. I'm sure, at all events, that that's what anyone coming suddenly upon the scene would have thought. The cry of 'Mad dog!' was taken up and passed from house to house, so that the news of my coming actually got ahead of me, and soon I found myself beset behind and before. People leaned out of second-story windows and threw flower-pots at me off the sills as I passed; policemen shot at me with pistols; one fellow tried to lasso me with a rope; another drove a big van across the road to head me off. Every man's hand was against me.

"But somehow, through the whole gantlet, I wriggled and darted and jumped and squirmed. In my excitement I swallowed my shaving soap, which made me feel deathly ill, but, of course, I couldn't stop.

"Luckily for me, the noise and hubbub had brought the Doctor to his gate before I got there. And as soon as he saw it was me that was being chased he opened the gate, let me slip in and closed it behind me. Bullets and buckshot spattered against the stone coping of the wall as I sped up the steps, across the garden and into the house. The Doctor—I wonder he wasn't killed himself—raised his hands in truce and walked halfway down the steps to meet my pursuers.

" 'That dog is mad!' yelled one of the gardeners rushing up with a gun. 'What did you let him into your house for? He might bite someone!'

"Of course in less than five minutes there was a crowd around the foot of the steps like a theater crush. Everybody talked at once. Some demanded that I be brought out and shot at once. And just as it began to look as though the crowd might thrust John Dolittle aside and take the law into its own hands my mistress arrived with her husband and a whole army of men servants.

"Of course the Doctor had guessed right away that I was

pretending—even before I gasped it out as I sped by him up the steps. He planted himself firmly in front of the closed gate and faced Oswald the husband, who had now, with a dozen flunkeys at his back, become very brave.

" 'You have my dog, sir!' said he, shaking his fist in the Doctor's face. 'The dog is mad. It bit my wife and several of the servants. It must be destroyed at once. Let us in, please.'

" 'Pardon me,' said the Doctor very politely—I was listening in great anxiety just below the study window—'the dog may be yours, but these premises are mine. You cannot come in. Now just calm down a moment and let us talk this over.'

" 'I will not listen to you,' cried the valiant Oswald. 'The dog is a danger to public health. It must be destroyed. It bit my wife who, in spite of her injury, has come here to see that no one else is harmed. The dog must be destroyed at once—immediately.' "

CHAPTER FOUR

THE DOCTOR GIVES A LECTURE

"By this time the crowd had grown still larger, all the stragglers having come up to be in at the kill. And things began to look really serious for the Doctor. A couple of old farmers in the rear began to harangue the mob, encouraging them to rush the gate. From my hiding place behind the study window I saw the crowd surge forward suddenly. I was still panting, breathless, from my long run. And the prospect of having to break out at the back of the house and be chased some more was not at all pleasant.

"But the Doctor wasn't to be easily brushed aside. He suddenly snatched a gun from the hands of one of the gardeners, and, bringing it to his shoulder, he faced the mob.

" 'Stand back—everybody!' he commanded shortly. 'This is my home and no one can enter it without a searchwarrant signed by a magistate.'

"At that, greatly impressed, the mob fell back instantly. I wondered what was going to happen next. But before the Doctor could say any more my mistress suddenly fainted into her husband's arms. I suppose she had just remembered how seriously she'd been wounded. Anyway, she nearly squashed poor Oswald, who was a small, frail man, with her enormous weight.

"That took the general attention off the 'mad dog' for the moment. The Doctor, calling to Dab-Dab to bring some water from the house, personally attended to the lady and she was soon brought round.

"Then he gave her a lecture. He assured her as a doctor and a veterinary surgeon that I wasn't mad at all. He told her kindly but firmly that she didn't know anything whatever about bringing up dogs—that he was well acquainted with me and was sure that she had ruined my disposition by turning me from a sporting outdoor dog into a silly boudoir pet.

" 'So you see, Madam,' he concluded, 'instead of being mad or having rabies, Dapple has merely started the habit of—er—hysterics—which, in fact, he has caught from you. Hysterics, Madam, you should know, while a very minor disorder, are highly contagious.'

"Some of the policemen had now arrived. And the farmers

had been urging them to go in and get me. But when it became known that the little man defending his home with such firmness was a Doctor of Medicine, a veterinary sur-

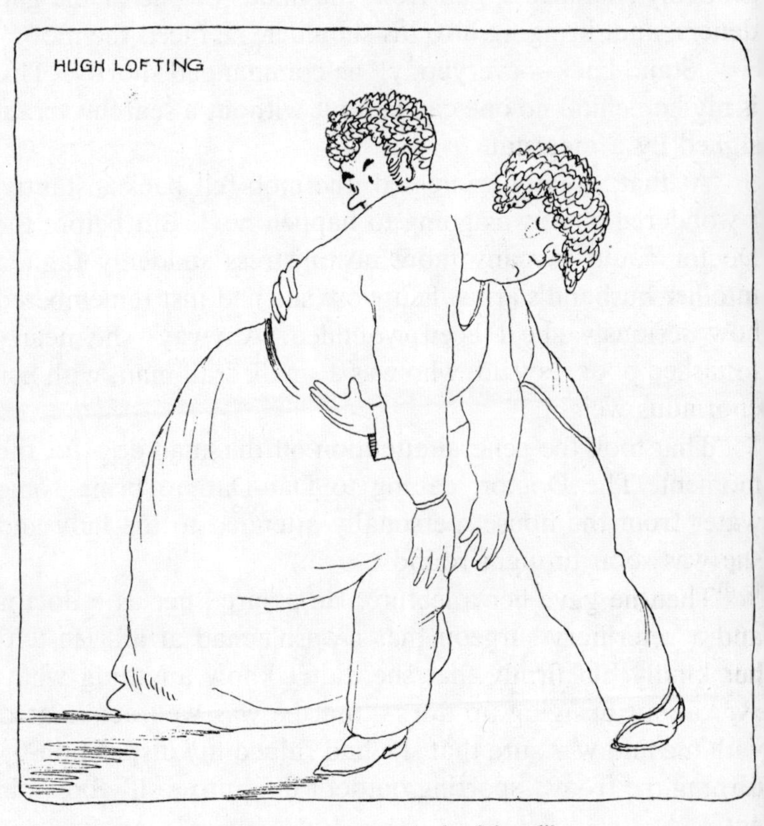

"My mistress suddenly fainted"

geon and a naturalist of great renown, the attitude of the whole crowd became entirely different. With such an authority maintaining that I was *not* mad, who would dare to invade his home and shoot me?

" 'I am quite willing,' said the Doctor, turning to the policemen, 'to assume entire responsibility for the dog—provided this lady will leave him in my care. And I think, Madam,' he added, addressing my mistress, 'that you have had abundant proof that the dog does not like the home you have given him. This, as you know, is the fourth or fifth time that he has run away and come to me for refuge. Don't you think that it would be more humane and best from all points of view if you left him here?'

" 'For my part,' Oswald began, suddenly recovering from his squashing, 'I wouldn't have the wretched cur in the house again for anything. I would sooner' . . .

"His enormous wife turned and glowered on him and the poor little man shriveled and subsided.

" 'Oswald,' said she, 'this is my affair.' She turned to the Doctor. 'I am very disappointed in the dog,' she said. 'He was sold to me as a thoroughbred. He couldn't have been that to prefer such a place as this'—with a magnificent gesture she waved a fat arm toward the Doctor's small and modest house—'to my home. I never wish to set eyes on the ungrateful creature again. I couldn't have treated a child of my own with greater kindness.'

"She began to weep.

" 'But don't you see?' said the Doctor, advancing toward her full of sympathy. 'That was just the trouble. You were too kind to him. He didn't want to be spoiled. He wished to be himself. He'—

"The woman waved him aside.

" 'Enough!' she cried. 'You may keep him. I never wish to see the ungrateful creature again—Oswald, lead me to my carriage.'

"And thereupon behind the curtain of the study window,

I threw a sommersault for sheer joy as the portly lady got into her victoria and drove away—for good—leaving me in John Dolittle's home . . . I am quite myself again now. But I believe I'd have become a real mad dog if I had stayed with her much longer . . . truly the Doctor is a great man."

The Dog Ambulance

CHAPTER ONE

THE FIRST PATIENT

IT WAS ABOUT this time that the Dog Ambulance was started. This institution (the idea, you may remember, was originally Jip's) belonged to and was organized entirely by the Club. It was the first thing of its kind in history. And I felt that a description of it and the events that accompanied its inauguration could quite fittingly be included in my book, *Tales of the Home for Crossbred Dogs*. On consulting Jip I found that he agreed with me and we decided to put it in following the Dalmatian's story.

For several days in succession we had had serious cases of dog casualities on the streets: dogs run over; dogs kicked by horses; sick and homeless strays, etc. Many of these cases when brought to the surgery were so far gone that the Doctor had a hard time pulling them through.

"Tommy," said Jip, coming to me at breakfast one morning, "we've got to have a dog ambulance. I'm sure we can get the Doctor to agree to it because I've already spoken to him about it—the time we brought Kling here when he was poisoned—and he thought it was a good idea. In the Home we have a couple of mongrel greyhounds. They're kind of funny to look at, but they're awful speedy. They have already volunteered to take it in turns doing duty. So we will have no difficulty with that part of it. What we need is the ambulance carriage itself and some harness for the greyhounds. Do you think you could build us a carriage and get your father to make us a set of harness?"

"Well, Jip," I said, "I don't know. But I am quite willing to try."

So that same evening I went over to the Stubbins' cobbler shop where I found that my father, though he was pretty busy, would make us the harness in his spare time. Then I set to work with Bumpo, the African Prince, who prided himself on being something of a mechanic, and out of a pair of rubber-tired perambulator wheels, a few springs out of an old bed and some pieces of packing-case, we constructed a very decent looking runabout, light enough to be drawn by a dog. We painted it white, put a red-cross flag on it and a bell. It was quite an elegant turnout.

When the harness was ready we hitched up one of the mongrel greyhounds, and Jip, as assistant casualty surgeon, drove around the zoo enclosure at a speed of thirty miles an hour—greatly to the astonishment of the inhabitants of Animal Town.

All concerned were very proud of the new Dog Ambulance. Night and day, from then on, one of the greyhounds was kept harnessed up in readiness to answer an emergency call.

"That's fine, Tommy," said Jip—"something that was really needed. Those serious cases can be brought to the surgery now with the least possible delay."

Well, as such things often happen, now that we had a brand-new Dog Ambulance ready for all emergencies, we got no cases to try it out on. Suddenly all dog casualities seemed to cease. The gallant greyhound steeds stood in the harness from dawn to dark and never a call came for their services.

Jip, Kling and Toby, the chief organizers of the Animal

It was quite an elegant turnout

Town First Aid, were dreadfully disappointed. Finally Jip became so anxious to try out the new ambulance that he and Toby decided secretly between them that if no case came along soon they would have to make one.

After many days of idle waiting they had (without telling either the Doctor or me) proudly led their ambulance out through the streets of Puddleby on their own. This they

He was a great garbage-heap explorer

did partly because they wanted the townsfolk to see the elegant equipage in all its glory, and partly because they might find a "case" by chance to try it on.

While they were parading through the town they came

upon Gub-Gub, the Doctor's pet pig, in a back street sitting on a garbage heap. He was a great garbage-heap explorer, was Gub-Gub. The poor pig had eaten some bad turnips and was looking rather green in the face from a slight stomach-ache.

"Ah! A serious case!" cried Jip, rushing the ambulance up alongside the garbage heap in grand style. Then with great dispatch Orderlies Kling and Toby, under the direction of Surgeon Jip, pounced upon the wretched Gub-Gub and began hauling him onto the ambulance. They would have sooner had a dog patient to try their new equipment on, but a pig was better than nothing.

"Leave me alone!" bawled Gub-Gub, kicking out in all directions. "I've only got a stomach-ache. I don't want to go on your ambulance!"

"Don't listen to him," ordered Jip. "He's delirious. Appendicitis most likely. It's a rush case, men. Get him on quick!"

The three of them rolled Gub-Gub's portly carcass onto the ambulance. Jip sprang into the driver's seat while Toby and Kling sat on the "delirious" patient to hold him down.

Like a shot out of a gun the mongrel greyhound bounded away at full speed for the Doctor's home. Meanwhile Jip clanged the bell for all he was worth to clear the road ahead and drown the bellowings of the first case to be brought to the Dolittle surgery by the Dog Ambulance.

CHAPTER TWO

THE MISHAP AT KINGSBRIDGE

It was a thrilling ride—thrilling for the staff of the ambulance, for the townsfolk who looked on and, most of all, for the patient. Certainly all records established up to that date were easily broken so far as sheer speed was concerned. But as to time—from picking up a case to delivery at hospital—that was another matter. Indeed, the original case never reached the surgery at all—in the ambulance. But I must tell the story in the proper order.

Streaking up the High Street with clanging bell, the strange vehicle shot under horses' noses, past traffic policemen who ordered it to stop, round corners on two wheels, scattering scared pedestrians right and left. At Kingsbridge it met with its first accident. Here the road narrowed as it crossed the river. In trying to avoid a peddler's barrow the greyhound steed went a shade too near a lamp-post. With Gub-Gub's extra heavy weight added to that of the two orderlies and the surgeon, the springs of the ambulance were being taxed to their utmost anyway. The hub of the right rear wheel only just touched the base of the lamp-post. But it was enough to throw the overloaded, careening carriage off its balance. On one wheel it shot across the road and dumped its entire contents, surgeon, orderlies and patient, over the parapet of the bridge.

As it happened, the river was at low tide. At such time,

wide stretches of black mud margined the narrow, swiftly running stream. This in a way was providential—for the patient, but not for the staff. Gub-Gub's rating as a swim-

. . . dumped its entire contents over the parapet

mer was very low, and had the river been at high tide he would have had a hard time reaching the bank. Jip, Kling and Toby, on the other hand, would have much preferred a clean bath to the fate that awaited them below the bridge.

All four landed with an oozy splash into the tidal mud. It broke the fall nicely, but it didn't improve their appearance. Entirely black from head to foot, the gallant staff still remembered its duty to the injured and proceeded to dig the struggling, squealing patient out of his mud bath.

Fortunately, the distance to firmer ground was not more than a few yards. Somehow the patient, who on account of his weight had sunk deeper in than the others, was hauled and dragged to solid territory. He may not have been a proper case for the ambulance when they had forcibly carried him off from the garbage heap, but by the time they had got him out of the mud of the river he was in considerably greater need of attention.

Regaining the bridge, the staff, now completely garbed in a new uniform of black mud, rolled the patient back onto the ambulance, jumped in after him and went away as fast as ever. In fact, they went even faster, for their mishap at the river had caused quite a crowd to collect and they were afraid they might be stopped at any minute.

For about a mile all went well. But as they turned into the Oxenthorpe Road at full gallop they met with still another accident. A sleek, overfed Pomeranian was crossing the road with great dignity. Suddenly, seeing the extraordinary carriage bearing down upon him at thirty-five miles an hour, he lost what little wits he had, ran first this way and then that and finally wound up under the front wheels of the ambulance. The carriage did not entirely capsize, but it tipped up sufficiently as it went over him to shoot the patient out again—this time into the gutter. The fiery greyhound steed was brought to a standstill and that keen—perhaps too keen—medical student, Jip, ran back to take charge of the situation.

The patient was lying on his back in the gutter, his four trotters waving in the air, yelling blue murder. Up the middle of the road the fat Pomeranian was also lying on his

. . . carrying him like a puppy

back and howling—mostly with indignation and fright. Surgeon Jip and Orderlies Toby and Kling held a hasty professional consultation. The ambulance could hardly take both casualties. Their first duty was to their original patient.

On the other hand, the Dog Ambulance was originally intended for dogs, and here was a fine case ready at hand.

However, while the discussion was still going on, Gub-Gub, fearing he might have to continue his hazardous ride in the ambulance, suddenly sprang up and took to his heels. Sore as he was from his fall and his stomach-ache, he had had enough of Jip's first aid.

This solved the problem for the staff of the Dog Ambulance very nicely. Jip grabbed the Pomeranian by the scruff of the neck and, carrying him like a puppy, dumped him into the ambulance, sprang in once more and gave the word to go.

It wasn't until after the flying carriage had done another mile that he suddenly realized that he had left his two orderlies behind. But Kling and Toby, by putting on their best speed, came in on foot a very good second and third in the race for the surgery.

CHAPTER THREE

THE RECEPTION AT THE SURGERY

Jip, Kling and Toby were all sadly disappointed at the Doctor's reception of the Dog Ambulance the first time it returned from active service. I am bound to say that the equipage had lost much of its original smartness. The wheels were bent and wobbly, the bell post was twisted up like a corkscrew and the bell gone, the first aid box beneath the driver's seat had burst open and bandages were trailing from it in the dust of the road behind. As for the staff, caked with mud and dust from head to foot, well, you could just tell that they were dogs and that was all.

The patient, as soon as the ambulance came to a halt, got out of the stretcher without waiting for assistance and at once began a long and indignant speech to the Doctor. He accused Jip and his assistants of first knocking him down by reckless driving and then kidnapping him right in front of his own gate.

No sooner had he finished his tirade than his mistress, who had followed in a cab, appeared upon the scene and began another long accusation. She assured the Doctor that she had heard a good deal about him and his crazy wild animals and she meant to appeal to the police. Things had come to a pretty pass, she said, when a man trained a gang of dogs to kidnap and steal other dogs.

The Doctor was just getting ready to answer her when Gub-Gub arrived, howling like a lost child who had been punished for something he never did. He began the third discourse upon the wicked deeds of the Red Cross Brigade who had carried him off against his will, thrown him over a bridge into the river, then rushed him over bumpy streets a few more miles and finally pitched him out into the gutter.

By the end of the last of these speeches the staff of the Dog Ambulance was beginning to feel that its services in the public good had been somewhat misdirected and not wholly understood. The greyhound steed slunk away to the zoo enclosure, where Bumpo undid his harness and separated him from the dilapidated carriage. As for Jip, Kling and Toby, they made no attempt to explain to the Doctor, but went miserably down to the fish pond and washed the mud from themselves. Not a word was said till they were on their way back to supper. Then Jip broke the silence with, "We shouldn't have started with that ridiculous pig. He always puts a hoodoo on everything."

The Stunned Man

CHAPTER ONE

THE ROBBERY

KLING, who came to be known as the Detective Dog, lived at Doctor Dolittle's Home for Cross-bred Dogs.

Gub-Gub, who dearly loved a mystery, tried to get Kling started on some new plot, because he was anxious to see a real detective at work. And by chance his wish was presently granted in a rather peculiar way.

Jip, who had been nosing about the neighbourhood in search of a bone he'd buried and lost, came upon a man lying in the middle of the road, unconscious. He immediately routed us out of bed and led us to the stranger.

Once more fate had pushed John Dolittle, willynilly, into the affairs of his neighbours. For, of course, even if he had not been a doctor, he would not have refused first aid to the injured at his door. Bumpo, who was living with us at the time, and I, helped him carry the man in and lay him on the table in the surgery.

The man was not seriously injured, though from the tremendous bump on the back of his head I had at first thought he might be. The Doctor brought him round after a few moments. And the first thing he said when he opened his eyes was: "I've been robbed. A lot of money has been stolen from me."

"Ah!" said Gub-Gub, who was listening at the surgery

A man was lying in the middle of the road, unconscious

door, "the mystery of the stunned man. Good! I'll get Kling."

The man seemed from his appearance to be a groom or stableman of some kind. As soon as he had gathered his wits together a little he began pouring out the story of his troubles without waiting for any questioning or encouragement from the Doctor.

"I had forty pounds with me," he said, "what the boss had given me to take to the bank at Oxenthorpe. I had just stopped a minute to tie my bootlace outside your gate here when someone hit me a terrible blow on the head from behind. Then all was darkness till I woke up here. There will be an awful row when the boss finds out the money's gone. You'll stand by me, sir, won't you? You'll bear witness to what I say? Be you a doctor, sir?" he ended, looking round the surgery at the bandages and bottles.

"Er-yes, I'm a doctor," said John Dolittle. "But why be anxious? Your story will, no doubt, be believed—so long as you state it exactly as it happened. All we know is that we found you unconscious in the road. We can't bear witness to anything further than that. If you were robbed it is quite possible that the police may be able to get the money back for your employer."

Gub-Gub, the pig, emerged from under the surgery table and nudged the Doctor's leg.

"I've brought Kling," said he. "He'll soon solve this."

"No," whispered the Doctor quickly. "This is the police's affair, not ours. We will stay out of it."

"Well, you see," the man went on, "you never can tell. The boss might even say that I stole the money. But you'll stand by me, won't you, Doctor?"

"I'll do what I said," the Doctor answered, apparently somewhat annoyed. "I can't do any more. But don't be worried. Tell your employer the truth and I'm sure that everything will come out all right. Do you feel steady enough to walk now?"

The man got down from the table and tried a few paces.

"Yes," he said, "I reckon I can manage now. Thank you, Doctor. I'll be going. But maybe I'll have to call on you as a witness later."

"That's all right," said John Dolittle. "I'm very busy, but I'll be willing to state what little I know of the case. Do you want me to send a message to have them come fetch you?"

"No, thank you," said the man. "I can walk."

As we followed the man out into the garden and watched him descend the steps, I noticed that Kling and Jip were examining the road opposite the gate with great care. Gub-Gub, deeply interested in the proceedings, was looking on. But the two dogs made him keep his distance; they were evidently anxious that no meddling pig's trotters should spoil the tracks in the dust.

Directly the man had disappeared the Doctor hurried away to his study to get in a few minutes' work at his books before breakfast; while I, to kill time till Dab-Dab, The Duck-Housekeeper, should summon us to the kitchen, strolled down onto the road to watch the detective dog's investigations. Jip came up to me as I reached the foot of the steps and spoke in whispers, looking backward over his shoulder with respectful awe at Kling, the great expert.

"He's marvelous, Tommy," he said—"simply marvelous. He has already found out that half what that fellow told us wasn't true and that there were a whole lot of other things he didn't tell us at all. For one, he had a horse with him."

"Goodness! Perhaps he was a highwayman," put in Gub-Gub, who had sneaked up and joined us. Jip ignored the remark with contempt.

"I thought I was pretty good at tracks myself," he went

on. "But compared with Kling, I'm just a beginner. On this case he hasn't said very much so far. But it's my opinion that he already has the whole thing straightened out in his mind."

As a matter of fact Kling, since he had left the police service in Belgium, had not, he admitted, had any desire to return to that kind of work. It was now quite clear to me that the flattering admiration of Gub-Gub and Jip had been too much for the famous dog detective and had got him started on his old profession again. After breakfast the two dogs disappeared (no doubt on business connected with "the case"); and it did not seem to me that any harm could be done so long as they didn't drag the Doctor into it.

But the next morning Dab-Dab woke me up in a great state of indignation.

"Tommy," said she, "you must make those wretched dogs stop this detective rubbish. What do you think they've done now?"

"I've no idea, Dab-Dab," I said, sitting up and rubbing my eyes sleepily—"No idea at all."

"Well, come down to the porch and look," said she.

Still only partly awake, I threw on some clothes and followed her downstairs.

"Open the front door," said she.

I did so. And an enormous pile of old, disreputable-looking shoes, which had evidently been stacked up against the door, spilled into the hall. While up the path from the gate Jip and Kling were just arriving, each with another old shoe in his mouth, to add to the pile they had collected.

"Good gracious, Kling!" I cried. "What's this? Any one would think that the Doctor had gone into the second-hand clothes business from the mess you've made of the porch."

"Sh! Tommy," whispered Jip. "Close the door and come outside a minute. Kling will explain."

"Explain! Rubbish!" squawked Dab-Dab angrily. "Kling just brought those shoes here to chew. He's as bad as Gub-Gub and his vegetable mysteries. If you dogs don't clear that mess off my porch before breakfast you won't get any—no, nor any lunch either," she added, as I closed the door on her wrath and followed the dogs down the path.

CHAPTER TWO

THE FOOTPRINT IN THE COPSE

Without further word the two of them led me out on to the road, turned to the right and took me about a quarter of a mile in the direction of Oxenthorpe. Then, through a farm gate, they jumped into a meadow and struck out across it toward a copse in the middle. Looking around to make sure that no one should see us enter, they finally led me into this through a hole in the surrounding hedge. Inside there was a clear open space beneath the trees where the earth was damp, mossy and practically grassless.

"This," said Kling, leading me across to the foot of an oak tree, "is where the money was buried. In fact, there is the money itself—in that bag."

The earth here was all dug up where the dogs had evidently rooted down following a scent. Among the loose earth there was a small linen bag. I picked it up and shook it. It jingled with the sound of gold.

"Now, Tommy," said Kling, "come over here."

I followed him a few yards away from the tree to where

a mossy hollow spread its green freshness beneath tall over-hanging hawthorns. It was a place which in wetter weather would have been a pond or bog.

It jingled with the sound of gold

"You see that? asked Kling, pointing with his nose.

"Yes," said I, "a footprint."

"Well, that's what we collected the shoes for," said he. "We want a shoe to fit that print."

"But how on earth," I asked, "do you expect to find it—out of all the shoes in the world?"

"We don't" said Kling with the patient air of a professor arguing with an obstinate, stupid child. "We don't expect to find it among all the shoes in the world, but only among the shoes that were thrown away last night in this immediate neighbourhood. Which is a very different matter. We know that the man who made this print threw his shoes away, because when we followed up the tracks and scent we found that he had done part of his journey in stockinged feet. That's why we've gone round collecting all the shoes we could find under hedges and everywhere. And now we want you to pick out from the pile we've gathered a shoe that fits that print."

"But why, Kling," I asked, "would not the scent you followed have led you to the man, even more surely than your knowing who it was that made this footprint?"

"Scents are freakish things," said Kling frowning. "It was clear and distinct this far and led us, as easy as pie, to where the money was buried—and even beyond it for a way. But we lost it about a half-mile from here. We lost the stocking-feet tracks, too. The man, whoever he was, knew something about covering his own trail—probably an old criminal."

"Then you don't think that the fellow that Jip found in the road could have hidden the money himself?" I asked.

"Certainly not," said Kling quickly. "We made a note of his scent when he was in the surgery. Whether he was in partnership with the man who took the money away and buried it, I have yet to find out. I suspect he was. Because the story he told the Doctor was *not* a frank statement at all. But he was not the one who brought the money here and buried it. That was done by the party who made that footprint. And then, I imagine, realizing that he had left tracks behind him, he got scared, took his shoes off and threw them away."

"But how do you know that he threw them away?" said I. "Why couldn't he have carried them in his hand?"

"Of that," said Kling, "we are not as yet absolutely sure. But we are pretty certain. For one thing, if he was afraid of the tracks giving him away to the police—he had made a whole lot of footprints in a field close to where the man was struck down—he would be afraid to have the shoes in his home. For another, he was already burdened with a spade, and perhaps other tools to do his digging with. It is certain that he was not far from home or he would never have attempted to make the return journey in his stockinged feet."

"Do you think," I asked, "that he himself might have struck the man Jip found while quarreling over the gold or something?"

"Perhaps, but I don't think so," said Kling. "It is more likely, in my opinion, that he found the man lying in the road before Jip got there; that he at once became terrified, thinking him dead or dying, that he would be blamed for it—since his tracks were in the road leading to the man's body.

"And of course it is most likely," Kling went on, "that the next thing he'd think of, after covering his own tracks, would be the hiding of the money, either because that also would throw suspicion on him or because he hoped to come later and dig it up after the row had blown over. So one of the first things we have to do before we go away from here is to cover our own tracks, leave everything as we found it and set someone on guard in case the man returns. That, however, I fear there isn't much chance of his doing for a longish time. Still, good detectives leave no loop-holes. We'll get Toby or Swizzle to hide in the bushes here and watch."

"Then you think we had better leave the money where it is?" I asked.

"Oh, certainly," said Kling. "It will be quite safe so long as we have one of the dogs watching. And we will be much more likely to find out things if we don't let on to what we already know. The best detectives always pretend to be as ignorant and as stupid as possible."

So, thereupon we proceeded to set the stage in the copse just as we found it. Kling, realizing that he probably had an experienced criminal to deal with, took the greatest pains to make sure that we left no trace to show that we had been there. After the earth had been put back into the hole on top of the money-bag he went over all the ground inside the copse slowly and carefully. Wherever the moss or the little under-shrubs had been beaten down by our feet he sraightened everything up to wipe out all traces. He even examined the encircling hawthorns lest we might have broken any leaves or left limbs drawn back showing where we had come through.

"I'll bring Swizzle and Toby up here as soon as we get back," said he, as we struck off across the fields for the gate. "They can take it in turns to keep watch."

Before leaving I had taken a rough tracing of the footprint with a pencil and paper, so as to be able to get an idea of which shoes might fit. Of course it wasn't very accurate, but I calculated that with its aid I could cut down the number of shoes I must bring up here to try—even if I did not succeed in making sure at the house.

CHAPTER THREE

THE SHOE THAT FITTED THE FOOTPRINT

On our way back, as we approached the Doctor's house, we saw three men descending the steps. The Doctor was standing at the gate at the top watching them. He looked worried and puzzled.

Kling at once shot off and overtook the men. He pretended to be doing nothing in particular; but I noticed by the way he stopped and sniffed in passing them that he was looking for a scent he knew.

"Who are those men, Doctor?" I asked as I joined him and walked up the garden path towards the front door.

"Oh, bother it, Stubbins!" said he rather irritably, "I don't know and I don't want to know. It is something in connection with this man we found stunned in the roadway—and the money that was missing. Those two big fellows are plain-clothes men, or private detectives or something of the sort. They wanted to know if I could identify the little man they have with them. He is under arrest, it seems, on suspicion of having done the deed. They asked me when I had seen him last. I never saw him before—thank goodness! I've no idea who he is."

"But I have, Doctor," said a voice behind us. And turning we found Matthew Mugg, who had mysteriously appeared from somewhere in the garden and joined us.

"That little bloke was Tobias Wilkes," he went on. "I know him well."

"But I don't," the Doctor put in hurriedly. "What on earth are all those shoes on the front steps for?"

"Oh, Kling is doing some investigating on his own account," said I. "He thinks he can find out who struck the man."

"Good gracious!" cried the Doctor. "For pity's sake don't let us have any more mysteries or detective work around here! Haven't we had enough already?"

And leaving us abruptly he fairly ran round the house to the side door to return to his work at which he had been interrupted.

"It'll go hard with poor Tobias," said Matthew thoughtfully as he watched the Doctor's figure disappear, "if he can't prove that he was somewhere else that night. His reputation's none too good anyhow. The Doctor's fibbing when he says he never saw him before—unless he has forgotten, convenient-like maybe. Why, he caught Tobias poaching pheasants not over a month ago. That I know, because I was helping Tobias myself at the time—only the Doctor never saw me."

As I climbed over the pile of old shoes and opened the front door Kling ran up to me.

"Tommy," said he, "I'd like to see you alone a moment."

"Well, Kling," I said when we were within the hall with the door closed behind us, "what is it? Was that little fellow the man who hid the money? I saw you sniffing at him as you passed."

"No, of course he isn't," said Kling impatiently. "Those lanky detectives are just plainclothes fools. This man smells entirely different. The fellow who made that footprint in the copse was the one who hid the money. What I want you to do now, Tommy, is to find the right shoe, if you can, among that pile. I've got to take Toby and Swizzle up to the copse and put them on guard. Blackie and Grab are keen to do it, but I'm afraid of fighting dogs for a job of this kind. They'd go for the man if he came, I know. All we want is small, clever dogs who will follow the fellow and see where he takes the money. So hurry up, will you? Now they've got the wrong man under arrest we've got to get busy."

Immediately he had gone I set to work with my tracing. Most of the pile of shoes were far too large or too small to leave any doubt. But one pair fitted suspiciously well. Jip was watching me with great interest.

"I remember where we found that pair," he said. "It was in a ditch at the bottom of the field where the copse is. Let's follow Kling up there right away and try it in the footprint itself."

So away we went without further delay.

We found the Dog Detective giving final instructions to his able lieutenants, Toby and Swizzle. He was very carefully repeating to them for the second time the exact place and manner they were to lie hidden and how they were to change guard at intervals. Swizzle, the clown dog, was taking it all as a joke; but Toby, the self-important, was treating it very seriously.

It was a thrilling moment when we laid the shoes over the footprint. It couldn't have fitted better.

"Good!" muttered the Dog Detective. "That is a big step in the chain of evidence."

"But, Kling," I said, "I don't see how you're going to find the man even now that you are sure that you've got his shoe."

"No," said Kling with some condescension, "having no experience as a criminal investigator, you wouldn't. But you see, I already have my suspicions—and an idea of where to look for my man. In fact, I am pretty certain—by guesswork it is true—of where the man lives. But several men live in the same place. With this shoe I can now tell which of the men it was who hid the money."

"Good gracious!" I said. "I had no idea that you had got that far. And where does the man live, might I ask?"

"He lives," said the Detective Dog, "at least I strongly suspect he does—in the same place as the stunned man lives; in the stable hands' quarters up at Squire Jenkins's place. If you will come with me we will now proceed there and continue our investigations."

I knew Squire Jenkins's place quite well. It was about two miles down the Oxenthorpe Road from the Doctor's house. Here in a fine old Georgian mansion the Squire (who many years ago had been one of the Doctor's patients) kept a large establishment with hunting stables, foxhound kennels and all the other things that in those days went with a big country house.

Around the wide yard behind the main building were the quarters for the grooms and stable hands—of which the Squire kept at least a dozen. This yard was reached by a private road whose gate was always open.

"It is my idea," said Kling as we reached the gate, "to drop the shoe in the middle of the yard and then retire to see what happens. We may have luck; we may not. We shall see."

I hardly expected that any one would object to my going down the private road. But I thought it best to make myself as little noticeable as possible in any case. I knew that no one would be likely to interfere with Kling.

Unchallenged, we got into the yard, where I lounged behind a hay-cart and watched Kling take his shoe out into the middle and drop it. Then he went smelling around just like any stray dog looking for rats.

From time to time various grooms and boys crossed the yard engaged on stable business of one kind or another. All passed the shoe with barely a glance.

But finally a lanky sort of a man with a very disagreeable face came out of a stable door carrying a saddle under his arm. The shoe lay right in his path as he crossed from that corner of the yard to the opposite. As his eye fell on it he gave quite a start. Then, glancing round nervously to make sure no one saw him, he hastily snatched it up from the ground, hid it under the saddle and hurried on. Kling, who had appeared to be examining a gutter the other side of the yard trotted carelessly across his path, sniffing, before the man disappeared into what seemed to be the harness room.

Then he dawdled around to my side of the hay-cart.

"Did you get a good look at his face, Tommy?" he whispered.

"Yes," I said, "I'd know him again anywhere."

"Good!" whispered the Dog Detective, pretending to scent another rat, "Then let's be going, shall we?"

CHAPTER FOUR

THE DOG DETECTIVE CONTEMPLATES

Without further words we left the yard together and made our way down the private road. At the outer gate Jip joined us.

"Well, Kling," I said, after we had tramped about half a mile in silence, "what is the next move?"

The Dog Detective, deep in contemplation, made no response.

"Sh!" said Jip. "Don't disturb him. He's thinking. Sometimes over his knottiest cases he goes into these moods for hours—and days—at a time. He'll speak when he's ready."

And Jip was quite right. Kling did not speak for another two and half hours. As soon as he got home he took out one of his old chewing shoes onto the lawn. There the reverie of the great investigator continued, while Jip and I sat around with our mouths open, wondering when he would have done enough thinking—and chewing—to say a little something. In this Gub-Gub came and joined us—though Jip was quite firm in making him keep his distance from the meditating detective.

"You've no idea, Tommy," he whispered to me, "what a time we've had with that ridiculous hog. He is just determined to follow this case inch by inch. There were moments when we simply had to run to get away from him. You can imagine how much chance two Secret Service Dogs like us would stand of finding out anything with a large grunting pig lumbering along behind us everywhere we went. I managed to shut him into the tool shed once, but he bellowed so loud that the Doctor thought some one was being killed and came running out from his study to see what was the matter— Goodness! Look at Kling. I believe he has found it."

The Dog Detective had ceased his thoughtful chewing. He was staring, motionless, at the lawn between his feet.

"I wonder," we heard him mutter to himself at last, "I wonder. It's possible—quite probable, in fact . . . Humph!"

Then suddenly he threw the boot aside, sprang up and disappeared out of the gate leading down the steps onto the road. Jip and I followed him running. So did Gub-Gub—greatly to Jip's annoyance.

In the road outside the gate the great investigator proceeded to run back and forth over the scene of the crime.

"Yes," he hissed at last, "it was—I'll bet my last boot it was . . . Tommy, our next job is to find a horse . . . a horse . . . a horse whose off hind-shoe has a bent nail in it."

"Why?" I asked. "What do you want him for?"

"Because he is the one who stunned the man," said Kling.

"Goodness me!" I cried. "You don't say! Kicked him senseless, do you mean?"

"No, that's the diddling point," said Kling. "He *didn't* kick him—of that I'm certain. And yet I'm positive that he is the only one who could have stunned the man. But how the dickens he did it I've yet to find out."

After a few moments of thought Kling turned back to me.

"Tommy," said he, "I think I'll get you to go down to those stables and do a little inquiring among the hands. If you get them chatting they will, maybe, tell you things which

I, of course, couldn't learn—that way—unless I talked their language. Meantime I've got some other business in connection with the case to attend to alone. Oh, and Jip, listen!

Suddenly he threw the boot aside

You might go up to the copse and see if Toby or Swizzle have anything to report."

Having thus given his assistants their orders, Chief Kling trotted away on his own affairs.

I proceeded at once to the Squire's place, where I strolled leisurely into the stable yard and tried to engage some of the hands in friendly conversation. It wasn't very difficult. I soon found a lad polishing a snaffle bit who seemed glad to have someone to talk to while he worked. I began by making a few remarks about horses—on which subject he was anxious to show how much he knew. Then I steered the conversation on to the topic of the robbery. The affair had apparently upset the whole establishment quite a little. The man who had been stunned had been the Squire's second head groom. I gathered that he wasn't at all popular with the rest of the stable hands, who were almost pleased that he had been knocked on the head. But the fact that the roads around peaceful Puddleby were evidently not safe for a man to travel alone, was a very different matter and had caused considerable indignation.

"Still," the boy ended. "I reckon they got the right party in handcuffs now, sure enough. That fellow Tobias Wilkes will have hard work proving it wasn't him. Squire got two smart detectives down from London, private detectives. He don't trust the police of these parts, Squire don't—thinks they be all fools. But them London fellows didn't take long over making an arrest. And they say they can prove that Wilkes came along that road just about the time that Fred Langley got knocked on the head. And I'll warrant that before long they'll prove he struck the blow and took the money. But he's an artful dodger, that Wilkes. What beats me is how he hid the horse he stole. It's easy to hide a bag of sovereigns, but 'tain't so easy to hide a horse."

"Oh, was there a horse stolen, too?" I asked, trying hard not to show too much interest.

"Surely, there was," said the lad. "One of Squire's best

hacks; a chestnut mare. She wasn't very young, but she was as fine a mare as you could find in these parts. And she just disappeared after that night as though the earth had

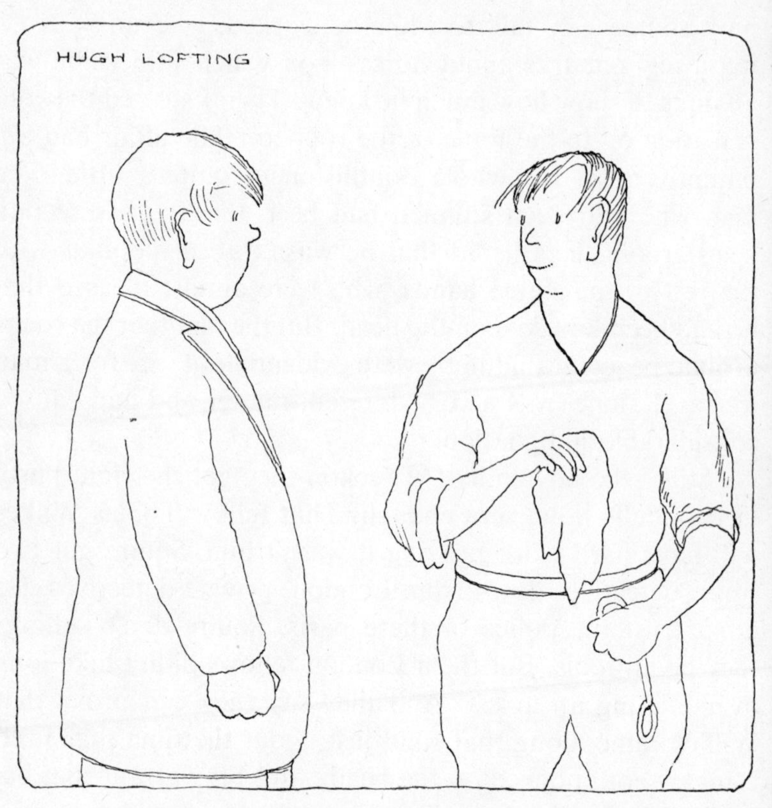

"Squire got two smart detectives down from London"

swallowed her up. Squire was more upset about her than he was about the money. She wasn't no hunter, but she was his favourite road hack and the cleverest horse, the prettiest pacer, I ever saw. Her name was Tiger Lily."

Before I left I learned that Langley, the man who had been stunned, was very friendly with the groom who had picked up the shoe. This fellow's name was Smedley. They happened to cross the yard together while I was still talking to the lad. Also I found out that Tiger Lily, the mare, was to have been shod at the Puddleby farriers the morning that she disappeared.

I felt quite proud, as I walked homeward, of my success. I found Kling waiting for me—also Matthew Mugg, who told me he had been making inquiries down in the town and had learned that the general opinion was that Tobias Wilkes would go to jail for a long term.

In a quiet corner of the garden, Kling, Jip and I held a little conference.

"We've got to hurry this thing along more than ever now, Kling," said I, "if we are to save Tobias from an unjust sentence."

"All right, all right," said Kling, "I know. The next thing is to find this mare, Tiger Lily. With her story—if we can get it from her, and I fancy the Doctor will be able to—the whole case will be complete. The Doctor doesn't want to be mixed in it, I know, but he will hardly refuse when we show him that it will save an innocent man from jail. I found a shoe which I am certain is Tiger Lily's about a mile along the road from where the man was struck down. I know it is hers because it had the bent nail in it which showed in the hoof marks not far from the Doctor's gate. Tracking her might have been possible if we had followed this clue the morning the man was found. But by this time, of course, with all the cart wheels and hoofs going over the road dust in the meantime, that is out of the question. What we need now is a dog with a peculiar gift in scent."

"How do you mean?" I asked.

"He means," said Jip, " a dog with a special nose for horses. Almost any dog is good on man scents. But one who can tell one horse from another by scent is pretty rare. Still, there are such dogs. Listen, Kling! Let's go down to the Home and see what we can do there."

Together the three of us crossed the big garden to the zoo inclosure. The Home for Crossbred Dogs happened to be just setting to on the evening meal. Jip at once went to the head of the center table and beat upon it for silence with a ham bone. The chatter and rattling of dishes ceased instantly.

"Members," said Jip, addressing the dining room in general, "we have particular and urgent need of a dog with a good nose for horses—one who can follow a single horse scent across the whole length of England, if need be. Is there any member present who thinks he could do that?"

CHAPTER FIVE

TIGER LILY'S TRAIL

Almost immediately after Jip ceased speaking a dog left the sideboard buffet where he had been helping himself to sausages and shambled forward through the crowd toward the speaker. He was indeed a sorry-looking animal. He had only one eye; he walked with a limp and seemed quite, quite old. I remembered him at once. He was a mongrel foxhound whom Jip had got into the club long after it was full, by using a lot of influence with the committee and the Doctor.

"Well, Mike," said Jip, as the veteran came to a halt at the center table, "do you think you could do it?"

"I don't think," said the old dog, swallowing half a sausage which he had brought with him from the sideboard, "I know I could. I was born in a hunting kennel. But because I wasn't thoroughbred they would never let me run with the pack. Still, I thought my nose was as good as any of 'em—even if I hadn't the speed and the looks. It was a dull life. There was hardly anything for me to do except hang around the stables, where the men used to laugh at me because I was crossbred. The hounds used to make fun of me too. One day I followed the pack anyway, even though the whips tried to beat me off. Of course I couldn't keep up the whole run, but I stuck with 'em for a good six or seven miles. Then I was blown. While I was resting, one of the huntsmen got thrown as he tried to jump a hedge. He was a parson, a nice old fellow who had often been kind to me. His horse took fright and bolted immediately, over the hills and far away. The idea came to me to try and follow this horse and find him for my friend the parson. And after I had got my wind back I up and after him. The whole countryside was, of course, full of the scents of horses. Just the same, I succeeded in singling this one out and trailing him down. I found him grazing fifteen miles away from the place he had spilled his rider. Then I knew I had an extraordinary and special scent for horses. And when I began to experiment and train it, I discovered that I could pick one horse out of a hundred with my eyes shut. It is a real gift, but, of course, no use in a foxhound kennel. To them hunting folk I was just a poor scrub mongrel, good for nothing. Have you got something I can take the scent from for this mare you have lost?"

"Yes," said Kling, "we've got a shoe. It hasn't been handled. I left it just where she dropped it."

"Good!" grunted Mike, "I'll find her all right. Just wait till I've eaten my sausages. I'll be with you in a minute."

And turning, the old veteran shambled back to the sideboard to finish his evening meal.

"Listen, Tommy," said Jip: "this is likely to be a long run. If we set out on it to-night you had better bring a supply of food and a blanket to sleep in. Goodness only knows how far old Mike may take us."

"All right," I said. "I'll go and get ready. When Mike has finished come and tell me."

Not wanting to worry the Doctor I merely told him that Jip, Kling and I were going out for a moonlight tramp and might not be home till late the next day. But I borrowed a little money from him in case we should need it. Then, by the time I had made up my bundle of the blanket and sandwiches, the three dogs were already waiting for me in the hall. Poor Gub-Gub tried very hard to join the party, but of course we couldn't take him.

The daylight was just starting to wane as we set out. Kling at once took us to the place where he had found the shoe. Old Mike sniffed at it, grunted and trotted off.

It was a strange journey and a strenuous one. Very soon I saw that with the coming darkness I stood a good chance of getting left behind. For the dogs, eager and long-winded, set a terrible pace at the start—in spite of old Mike's limp. Jip, after I had had to call to them more than once to wait for me, suggested that I tie a string to his collar so that I could keep in touch.

It seemed as though Tiger Lily had been pretty sure of her direction; for the scent hardly every halted or dawdled around. She had just hit across country, regardless almost of anything. There were places where she had evidently leapt high hedges, forded streams, swum lakes and waded bogs. More than a dozen times I was on the point of telling the dogs that they would have to go on alone to find the trail's end. But the thrill of the chase fascinated me and kept me going through it all.

About midnight I told them that I thought it was time we all took a rest for I saw that they, too, were pretty well winded. The four of us, therefore, ate a sandwich apiece, rolled ourselves in the blanket under a tree and went fast asleep.

Next morning, after another sandwich all round, we were up and going again through the dewy fields almost before the sun had arisen. Till now I had very little idea of where we were, beyond the guess that we had come in a north-easterly direction away from Puddleby, and had made about twenty miles. And even with the daylight I wasn't much the wiser. The dogs, from their conversation, seemed better acquainted with the neighbourhood than I was. One village which we skirted looked, however, vaguely familiar to me. I asked Jip if he knew the name of it.

"Yes," said he, "that's Digby Royal."

"Digby Royal," I muttered, "Curious! The name sounds familiar, too. Can I have been here before?"

And then it dawned on me that I had once on a journey with the Doctor changed coaches at a town of that name. I tried to remember what place we were going to on the journey. But that year the Doctor and I had done a good deal of traveling together about the country in pursuit of ferns, the study of which greatly interested him just then. Still, I thought, I ought to be able to remember.

For some hours, as we trudged along behind Mike, I cudgeled my brains, annoyed with my poor memory.

At last it came to me.

"Yes, that's Digby Royal"

"Jip," I cried, "I have an idea of where this trail may lead us."

"Where?" he called back.

"To the Retired Cab and Wagon Horses' Association," I

said. "I've just remembered where we were going when we last passed through Digby Royal."

"By jingo!" muttered Jip. "That's so. I've gone there

We found places where she had lain down

many times with the Doctor myself. And this is the way we always came. We're now approaching Bentlake. That's where the Doctor and I stopped for lunch last time. Humph! I wonder if you're right."

"Well," I said, "it is certain that the mare would have heard of the Doctor's home for retired horses, living as she does almost next door to John Dolittle's house. And it would be natural enough if she went off by herself, meaning to run away for good, that she would make for that as the best hiding place—in fact the only place where she would be safe from the interference of people."

Jip said no more but trotted on after Kling and Mike, wrapped in thought.

The trail artfully went around all the towns as though the mare (I remembered the stable lad's speaking of her extraordinary cleverness) had realized that she would be in danger of being stopped if she passed through streets with no one leading or riding her. On the way we found places where she had evidently lain down to hide from passers-by behind high hedges or in the sheltering refuge of a copse of wood.

I became quite interested in the prospect of meeting this highly intelligent horse. And I began thinking about what Kling had said: that he was sure she had stunned the man—but not by kicking him. Could she have known something about him, disliked him perhaps, and stunned him on purpose to escape. And, above all, how in the world had she done it?

CHAPTER SIX

TOGGLE'S SILENCE

As we drew nearer to the district where John Dolittle had established his now well-known Retired Cab and Wagon Horses' Association, Jip and I became surer than ever that my guess had been right. The hills and the farms round about were more familiar territory to me than much of the country nearer home. For I had spent many pleasant days here with the Doctor talking to Beppo and Toggle, the famous old plow horse with green spectacles.

At the main gate to the Rest Farm these two were standing, when we at last came in sight of it, almost as though they had been expecting someone's arrival. They were delighted to see Jip and myself. Of the other dogs, Kling and Mike, they seemed suspicious until we introduced them as part of our party.

Inside the lovely meadows we stretched ourselves beneath the giant elms and ate the last of our sandwiches. We were all weary and dead beat after our long journey.

When I came to question Toggle about the chestnut mare, to my great astonishment he first remained entirely silent. Then, evidently ill at ease, he assured me that no such horse had joined the association. He turned to old Beppo, who also gravely shook his head. Then Kling came up behind me and whispered in my ear:

"They've promised to say nothing. You can see that.

Tiger Lily must be here. Old Mike says her scent is all over the place. She's hiding behind a hedge or something."

"Well, couldn't Mike nose her out?" I whispered back.

Beppo and Toggle were at the main gate

"Better not," said Kling. "The chances are she would just jump a fence and bolt. And then we'd have another fifty-mile chase to catch up with her again. Let me talk to these old fellows. If the mare is scared it will be best to get them to make her listen to reason."

Thereupon Kling explained to Beppo and Toggle (who were the president and vice-president of the association) that, first of all, we were quite certain that the mare was here. Secondly, that it was wrong of her to try and stay hidden, because an innocent man was in danger of being sentenced for something he hadn't done; and to clear up the matter it was necessary to tell the police how Langley had been stunned. Also that the Squire, who valued the mare highly, would want to claim her, and the Doctor would get into trouble with him when it became known that she had taken refuge at the Dolittle Rest Farm.

"So you see," Kling ended, "it would be far better if you two went to Tiger Lily and persuaded her to come and have a talk with us. Tell her that Tommy will promise to make no attempt to capture her against her will. But we must see her."

Finally the two old horses seemed to see the sense and fairness of what Kling had proposed. They told us to stay where we were while they drew off a short distance and conferred together in whispers. A little later we saw them disappear behind some hedges and for a while we saw nothing more of them.

"I wouldn't wonder," Kling whispered, "if Tiger Lily has been listening all the time somewhere quite near. We've got to be careful how we handle this mare, Tommy. I've a notion she's full of what Bumpo calls temperamentality—skittish and wayward, you know. Look out! Here she comes."

I don't think I shall ever forget my first sight of Tiger Lily. For never had I seen a more beautiful, enchanting animal. She suddenly appeared in a gap in the hedge between the two old veterans. It may have been that their aged, broken-down look served to set off her clean, well-groomed, dainty grace. But as she stood there she seemed to me to have something of the almost supernatural about her. From her alert, clever eyes to her neat, slender fetlocks, she was a picture to warm the heart of any man.

"I wouldn't wonder if she has been listening," Kling whispered

It was very evident that though she had consented to come to the parley, she was not placing any great confidence in the promise that she would not be captured. At an easy supple walk she picked her way down the slope in our direction, but paused a good thirty paces from us and would come no nearer. I noticed those intelligent eyes taking in not only every detail of ourselves but glancing around and beyond to make sure that the way of escape would be easy if any attempt should be made upon her liberty.

As I got up to address her I felt a new and peculiar pride in my knowledge of horse language, since it enabled me to converse with a creature such as this.

"How do you do, Tiger Lily?" I said, smiling to reassure her. "I am glad that you consented to come and talk with us. Please have no fear. You are not among enemies. We come, as Toggle has no doubt told you, from John Dolittle's house. It is necessary, for the sake of a man who has been wrongly arrested for striking down Fred Langley, that we hear your story of the night and early morning when the thing happened. Won't you please tell us?"

The mare thought for a moment. Then she threw back her shapely head and blew gently through her silky nostrils. The white of her muzzle and a star between her eyes were the only spots that broke the even, glossy chestnut of her coat.

"Yes," she said at length. "I'll tell you the whole thing as far as I know it. But I will not come with you. So you can put that out of your minds right away."

CHAPTER SEVEN

HOW THE MARE GOT AWAY

I was disappointed at the mare's words. But before I had a chance to make any comment Kling whispered: "Don't try to persuade her now. Wait till she has told us her story. Let her get more confidence in us first. Take her easy."

"This thing goes back," Tiger Lily began, "quite a long way—to the time when the road hacks were a much more important part of the Squire's stables than they are now, when people used the roads more and these diabolical railway things which are doing their best to ruin the countryside, hadn't been invented. In those days most of the journeys that the Squire and his guests made were done on horseback. But later, when the hunters came to be almost the whole thing at the stables, I and a few hacks that were still kept were put into the stalls at the north end of the yard, and Langley, the second groom, was put in charge of us. Up to that time old George Gibbons, the head groom, had had the management of us, and things were different. The Squire is an easy-going man and a great deal went on in his stables that he never knew of. That fellow Langley is a low-down, cruel, thieving rat. You must excuse my language, but he deserves it, every bit. As soon as he was given sole charge of the hack stables, with the buying of the fodder and everything, he started to cheat the Squire right and left. He cheated us, too. He got the corn chandler to serve us with cheap, moldy oats, maize with worms in it and bad hay. And all the time he was charging the Squire for the best quality, which was what old Gibbons had always got for the stables.

"More than that, he was cruel. He never let the Squire see him, but when no one was around he was always beating us, kicking us and treating us abominably. There was another fellow almost as mean and low as himself, called Smedley."

(Kling here glanced at me and nodded significantly.)

"Langley made Smedley sort of second-in-command of the hack stables, and when one wasn't knocking us about and swearing at us the other was. Well, one day I noticed these two doing a good deal of whispering and confabbing together and I guessed that they were hatching some plot. All I hoped was that I wasn't going to be in it. But when Langley came and saddled me and took me out of my stall about two o'clock the next morning, I saw that I was going to be in it. It was evident that he meant to steal me—or that's what I feared at the time anyway—and it turned out later I was right. The prospect of being owned and ridden by that horrible man for the rest of my life was too awful for anything. And right away I began to look for a chance to escape from him."

Kling at this point moved restlessly in the grass as though impatient to hear whether the outcome of Tiger Lily's story fitted in with his own guesswork version of the case.

"Well," the mare went on after a moment, "Langley led me out through the yard, taking care to walk me always on the soft places so my hoofs would make no noise. Even after he reached the highway he seemed afraid to get up on my back, lest, I suppose, I should go away at a trot and wake some one in the stables. When he had come opposite the

Doctor's house he stopped. He had already been looking back a good deal. It seemed to me as though he were expecting some one to join him for he kept muttering words of

"I guess they were hatching some plot"

annoyance. After standing there a little while he started to go back along the road a short way, so that he could see around the bend. He didn't take me with him, fearing again, no doubt, the noise I might make in turning. But he had a long leading rein in his hand. It permitted him to get about five or six yards away from me. I thought of suddenly giving a tug, wrenching the rein out of his hand and bolting. But I saw he had it wound around his wrist and I was afraid to try it.

"He remained standing there a moment with his back to me. It seemed somehow the right time to make an attempt to get away. And while I was wondering how I'd go about it I felt one of my hind shoes, as I shifted my weight from one leg to the other, slip off my hoof into the dust of the road. This at once gave me an idea. From where I stood I could not reach to kick him. But if I could only throw that shoe accurately enough to hit him on the head with it the trick would be done. As it happened, when I was once in pasture with some other horses I had had a shoe come off and had amused them and myself by slipping it on again and throwing it quite long distances. It can be done, if you are only patient enough and a few of the old nails remain standing up in the shoe to get a hold by.

"It was a slim chance, but it was worth trying. I looked back over my shoulder and took careful aim. Langley was standing quite motionless, still looking down the road for his friend who didn't come. I pressed my hoof firmly down on to the shoe so I could pick it up. Then I drew up my right hind foot slowly and shot it out in the direction of Langley's head with all my force. The shoe skimmed through the air whistling and hit him on the head with a thud. He had his cap tilted well back, otherwise it would certainly have killed him. He dropped like a stone and lay still."

"Then what happened to the shoe?" asked Kling.

"It bounced off his head," said Tiger Lily, "and fell a good twenty feet distant. At first I was afraid of being tracked if I ran away with only three shoes, and I turned and went back for it. I pressed the nails well home into the old holes and managed to keep it on for a few hundred yards.

"The shoe hit him on the head with a thud"

Then, as I was jumping a hedge to get into a field, it came off again, and I saw it was hopeless to try and keep it any longer. So I just hit across country to come here."

"You never went up close to the man again after he fell?" asked Kling.

"No," the mare answered. "I only went around him to get the shoe, which lay off to the side of the road."

"That's how I knew you hadn't kicked him," said Kling. "Your standing backwards tracks were all too far away to reach him with a kick. But you dragged the man a little before you got clear, did you not?"

Tiger Lily's bright eyes opened wide as she looked at this mysterious dog who seemed to know everything.

"Yes," she said. "The leading rein was wound so tight about his wrist I couldn't get free. But I only dragged him a couple of feet before it slipped away. How on earth did you know?"

"Pshaw!" said Kling, tossing his head. "The track where he had been drawn along in the dust was as plain as a pikestaff. Now tell us, did you see anything of the man Smedley that night—or rather morning?"

"Yes," said Tiger Lily. "I can just say that I saw him. When I went back for the shoe I got a glimpse of him hurrying down the road. I'm pretty certain it was he. But, of course, I didn't wait till he came up. In fact, that's why I jumped the hedge. I didn't want anyone to see me and follow me . . . That is all of my story. Now I think I'll be going."

"Oh, but just a minute, Tiger Lily," said I. "Don't you see that your staying here is likely to make things very awkward for Doctor Dolittle? If you came back with us, it—"

"I am *not* coming back with you," the mare quickly interrupted, getting ready to bolt. "Nothing in the world would induce me to."

"Don't get her scared," whispered Kling. "All right," he said aloud, turning to the mare again. "We are not going to force you. But listen: if John Dolittle comes here will you speak with him?"

"Oh, certainly," said Tiger Lily—"of course."

"Very good then," said Kling. "Thank you very much for your information. Let us be going, Tommy."

And as soon as we had said good-bye to Toggle and Beppo we made our way out through the main gate.

CHAPTER EIGHT

NEWS FROM TOBY

"Humph!" said I as we started off along the road. "Just the same, we didn't do a bad night's work. We found the mare and we got her story . . . Poor old Doctor! It looks as though we shall have to drag him into it after all. Do you think she will come—even with him, Kling?"

"Oh, of course," said the Detective Dog. "All her panic is over those two low fellows, Langley and Smedley. I don't blame her myself. But, after all, she doesn't know us, and she is in a sort of hysterical state. But once the Doctor guarantees her that she won't have to have anything to do with those two, she'll come all right. I learned from some of the dogs around the stable yard that the Squire himself is very kind to his animals. And you heard her tell us that she was happy there until that horrible Langley got put in charge."

"I wonder what is the quickest way we can get back," said Jip. "Old Tobias Wilkes is the one that I'm thinking of. I wish we had something faster than our legs to carry us."

"Look here," I said. "I got a little money from the Doctor before I left. Let's hurry on to Digby Royal and see if we can't catch a coach from there. I think I have enough for the fare."

So, putting our best foot forward, we reached Digby Royal before noon. Luckily a coach was leaving at half-past one. After asking the cost of the journey I found that I had enough to buy us all a light lunch in addition—of which we were all more than glad.

We got back to Puddleby about tea time. Dab-Dab was very angry with us for not letting her know we would be away so long; and Gub-Gub was consumed with interest to know where we had been, what we had done and how much we had found out.

I waited till tea was over before I tackled John Dolittle on the subject of his going to interview Tiger Lily.

"You're the only one who can bring her back, Doctor," I said, after I had outlined the situation to him. "There's no doubt about that. And I'm really afraid that if the Squire's detectives get combing over the country they will find out where she's hiding and then they'll be after you. It would be best, I think, if you went and saw her right away and tried to make her listen to reason."

The poor Doctor, who was in the midst of a very important treatise on the subject of moths, looked up at me wearily, but said nothing.

"And besides," I added, "we need you to get Wilkes out of this. He's in a very serious situation."

Well, the Doctor finally saw, of course, that if he didn't take a hand in it, it was going to be a very complicated business for all concerned, and a decidedly grave one for Tobias Wilkes. When I had finished he sent me for Kling, and asked the Detective Dog to tell him his version of the story from beginning to end. After which he sat silent for a little, thinking.

While we were still waiting for him to speak we heard a

Toby sprang up on the sill

pattering of paws on the gravel outside the study window and suddenly Toby sprang up onto the sill.

"Kling!" he cried. "Someone came back after the money while I was on the watch. That fellow Smedley—from Squire Jenkins's place."

"Well, did you trail him?" asked the Detective Dog.

"Yes," said Toby. "And he came down the Oxenthorpe Road. I think he's going into Puddleby on foot. He has only just gone by our gate. But you'll have to hurry if you want to catch him."

In a moment the Doctor and I were out in the front garden and leaping down the steps. After us came not only Kling, Toby and Jip, but Blackie, the retriever, and Grab, the bulldog, as well. At a distance of not more than a couple of hundred yards from the gate we saw the figure of a man hurrying along towards the town as fast as he could go. He looked over his shoulder, and seeing us, put on even more speed—indeed he seemed about to break into a run.

"Go after him, Blackie," said the Doctor quietly. "Don't hurt him, but just get ahead of him and keep him where he is till we can catch up."

Blackie, followed by Grab and Jip, shot after the hurrying figure, which they promptly surrounded and brought to a standstill.

At first when the Doctor came up and spoke to him, Smedley's manner was a mixture of fear and brazenness. But after it had been explained to him that his partnership with Langley and all the other details of the case were well known to us, he was just terrified and nothing more. He started to excuse himself for his part of it, trying to throw the entire blame upon Langley. But the Doctor cut him short.

"There is only one thing that can save you from a heavy sentence," said he. "And that is that you do exactly as I tell you. To begin with, give me the money."

Smedley was evidently for a moment going to deny that he had it. But something about the Doctor's determined look and the fact that he already seemed to know everything, made him realize that that would be useless. Shamefacedly he brought the linen bag out of his pocket and handed it to the Doctor.

"The next thing," said John Dolittle, "go and get Langley and bring him to my house—that one there, with the steps leading up to it. If your friend should be unwilling to come just explain to him that it will cost him his liberty as well as yours. We have both your descriptions. You could not get far. If the two of you are not at my house within half an hour I will inform the police of all that I know."

CHAPTER NINE

TIGER LILY'S RETURN

As a precaution Kling dispatched his able lieutenant Toby to shadow Smedley when he left the Doctor's house. But this turned out to be unnecessary. Apparently Langley was quickly persuaded that it was wiser to fall in with the Doctor's orders than to try to get away, for less than twenty minutes later we saw the two men coming up the garden path. I opened the front door myself and took them at once to the Doctor's study.

Kling and I were the only others present at the interview. John Dolittle did not take long over it. In as few words as possible he showed them that the whole truth of the case was in his possession and what he now proposed to do.

"Much will depend," he ended, "on whether the Squire decides to drop the case or not. I am hoping for your sakes—though you richly deserve punishment—that I can persuade him to go no further with the matter if the money and the horse are restored to him. What I should recommend you to do is to go away from this district altogether and make a new start. And remember, if at any time you are tempted to go in for this sort of crooked game again, that your faces are well known to me and several witnesses here."

The two men, who had been very plainly terrified of what the Doctor might do, were quite overjoyed at this permission to escape. As a matter of fact, they wasted no time over it, but got out that same evening and were never seen again in the neighbourhood of Puddleby.

The Doctor's interview with the Squire was somewhat more difficult. Indeed, if the old Squire had not known John Dolittle so well it is doubtful if it would have been successful at all. But finally, after the Doctor had talked to him for quite a while, he agreed to withdraw his detectives from the case. And as it was they who had accused Tobias Wilkes, that was the end of that charge and Wilkes was released.

"And if, Squire," said the Doctor as he was leaving, "you should find that one, or perhaps two, of your stable hands suddenly depart from your employ, you will not make any attempt to trace them up, eh?"

At this the Squire looked sharply at his old friend and pondered a moment before answering. Finally he laughed.

"All right, Doctor," said he. "You know more than you're letting on to, I reckon. No, I'll go no further with the business. I've come out of it pretty well thanks to you. I've got the money back, and if you can find Tiger Lily for me I'll be glad enough to call it quits. Seems to me you've been to a peck of trouble on my account. Maybe the day will come when I can do something for you."

"The job now, Stubbins," said the Doctor as we came away from the Squire's house, "is to tackle Tiger Lily. I hope she will not be unreasonable. If she is, there will be nothing left but to buy her from the Squire and leave her at the Rest Farm. And goodness only knows how much that will cost . . . Well, we shall see."

The Doctor set out for the Rest Farm the following day and Kling and I accompanied him.

As a matter of fact, I was half hoping that the mare would refuse to return, because then there might be a possibility, when she had been bought by the Doctor, that I would sometime get a ride on her. I felt it must be great fun to ride a horse as clever as Tiger Lily.

As usual, a tremendous fuss was made over John Dolittle by all the members of the association when he arrived at the gate. And he was kept busy answering questions for a good half-hour before he had a chance to bring forward the matter of his own business.

One of the horses went off and brought Tiger Lily, who was still keeping to the secluded parts of the farm for fear any people passing on the road might recognize her. The difference between her manner with John Dolittle and that in which she had received me and Kling the other day was very noticeable. She seemed genuinely glad to see him and came right up to where he stood with all the confidence in the world.

Then very gently, just as though he were chatting about the weather or anything, he told her she need have no fear about going back because the two men she disliked had already left the Squire's employment, never to return. He promised her, moreover, that if the groom that took Langley's place wasn't to her liking, he himself would speak of it to the Squire, who would surely see that her complaints were attended to.

She listened thoughtfuly and at the end she said:

She listened thoughtfully

"All right, Doctor, I'll come. But I want you to promise me as well that when my riding days are over you will buy me from the Squire and let me come back here."

"Certainly," said the Doctor. "I feel pretty sure that the

Squire will consent to that. Now, did you bring a saddle with you?"

"Yes," said she. "But I rubbed it off against the scratching-post. I had to bite through the girths to do it. But I dare say you can patch it up for one journey."

To my great delight, the Doctor, who knew that I was crazy to ride the beautiful mare, suggested that I take her back while he and the dogs went by coach. Tiger Lily very graciously consented to this also—though she told me before the journey was over that I was about the worst horseman she had ever traveled under. Just the same, it was the grandest ride I ever had; and I learned more from her remarks on the way about "good hands" and a firm seat than I had ever known before.

When we were seated at supper that night (Dab-Dab had, among other things for us, a late crop of very wonderful green peas) Gub-Gub as usual demanded that we give an account of our day's doings. We told him that Tiger Lily had been brought back and restored to the Squire.

"But what about Tobias Wilkes?" he asked.

"Oh, I went down to the police station," said the Doctor, "with the Squire himself. Wilkes is already released from custody."

"Custardy!" grunted Gub-Gub, bringing his nose up out of a plate of peas. "Who's custardy?"

"No, it's nothing to do with custard," said Jip contemptuously. "The Doctor means that he is already released from jail. Your mind is just a food mind—as has been remarked before."

"Well, there are worse kinds of minds than food minds," said Gub-Gub. "Goodness! I wish I had brought my food spectacles to supper with me. These peas are so small I can hardly see them. Hump! So Wilkes is released and the mare returned. Then I suppose that's the end of the Mystery of the Stunned Man. Kling is a fine detective and it was an elegant mystery. I wonder what the next one will be?"

"There are not going to be any more," said the Doctor quickly.

"I should think not indeed!" snorted Dab-Dab, glowering indignantly upon Gub-Gub.

"After all a little mystery goes a long way," put in Chee-Chee, the monkey.

"In Africa,' said Polynesia, "there was a good deal too much mystery. On the other hand, it was a wonderful climate. I don't like the way that wind is wailing in the chimney. Heigh, ho! I suppose the summer's over already and the blithery, shivery time is beginning. I think I'll borrow one of the Doctor's socks and make a sweater out of it."

"But if we're not allowed to have any more mysteries and detective cases," said Gub-Gub, "what are we going to do for amusement the long winter nights. The Doctor is always too busy now to tell us stories round the fire."

"What are the animals talking about, Tommy?" asked Bumpo.

"The Doctor was just telling Gub-Gub that we'd had enough of mysteries and detective work," said I.

"Oh, deciduously so," said Bumpo, biting into an enormous slab of bread and treackle. "I never cared for an atmosmear of mystery."

"Listen, Stubbins," said the Doctor, "if you have finished I think we had better go over to the Home for Crossbred Dogs right away and speak to Kling before he gets started on a new problem of some kind. I really can't have any more interruptions. I am dreadfully behindhand with my book on moths."

"So am I—on my book," said Gub-Gub, pushing his plate forward for more peas.

"Your book!" screeched Too-Too. "What book are you writing, for pity's sake?"

"The History of Food," said Gub-Gub quietly—"a most important work. It's nearly done. I only have seven more volumes."

The Crested Screamers

CHAPTER ONE

REGENT'S PARK

WHEN Doctor Dolittle was preparing his Canary Opera to be shown in London he went to the Zoo in search of bird-singers and bird-dancers for the choruses. Cheapside, the London sparrow and Becky, his wife, went along to help. Gub-Gub, the pig, who assisted the Doctor in the production of the show was eager to be in on the casting.

"Can I go to the Zoo?" he asked.

"You can *not,*" snapped Cheapside. "Do you want to get us arrested? 'Ow far do you think the Doc would get with a full-sized porker afollowin' 'im through the crowd?"

So, much to poor Gub-Gub's disappointment at again being left behind, the Doctor finally set out with only the sparrows for company.

" 'Ow long is it since you was at the Zoo, Doctor?" asked Cheapside when, after forty-minutes' walk, they were beginning to approach the neighbourhood of Regent's Park.

"Oh, my!" said John Dolittle, "it must be—let me see—it must be more than two years now, Cheapside, since I was there."

"Humph!" said the sparrow with a knowing air. "I reckon you'll find it changed considerable. Much bigger. But you'll 'ave a better chance to see the kind of thing you want. The collection of birds 'ere is the best in Europe now."

"How do you know?" asked the Doctor.

"Oh, I've been around all the Zoological Gardens on the Continent," said Cheapside very grandly. "You know we used to live in Regent's Park, as I told you. And Becky, 'ere, has been pestering me ever since we left to go back there. But I always told 'er you can't beat St. Paul's. It's more central. One time she was at me so hard that I told 'er I'd take 'er on a trip around the Zoos of Europe—just to pacify 'er like. But when she come back she was more in love with Regent's Park than ever."

"What countries did you visit?" asked the Doctor.

"Pretty near all of 'em," sighed Cheapside. "We did a grand tour. But we was both glad to get back to London. Still, some of them furrin' cities wasn't so bad. They've got an awful big Zoo in 'Amburg and another in Hantwerp. But I didn't think much of them. I liked Paris. They've got a nice place there they call the Jardong day Plonks—fine lot of parrots and macaws. Noisy things. But the park I liked best in Paris was the Twiddle-didee Gardens, near the Lufer Palace. There's an old feller there—nobody knows 'ow old 'e is—who makes a specialty of feedin' the sparrers. 'E's done it for years. 'As 'is picture took regular, 'oldin' up 'is 'and with crumbs, and sparrers settling all over 'im. 'Course while me and Becky was in Paris, *we* got most of the crumbs. Them French sparrers ain't much good at fightin'. Some of them is so polite with their 'After you, sirs,' that I wonder they don't starve to death. I liked Paris pretty good. Becky 'ere said she thought it was a kind of frivolous place. From there we went on to Geneva, Switzerland—you know, where the cuckoo-clocks come from. There they've got a park, about the size of a back yard, what they calls the Jardong Onglays—that's the parley-voo for the English Garden. The cheek of 'im! There's nothing English about it. Ain't even got dandelions in it. From there we went on to Rome, Barcelona, Madrid and all the rest. We did a regular tour. But we was both glad to get back to dear old London."

"Yes," said Becky, "and you made straight for St. Paul's and settled down in the noisiest part of the city. That's all that travel did for you. Instead of broadening your mind, it made you narrower than ever. Who would want to make his home in the most crowded corner of the city—right on top of the Royal Exchange—when there's Regent's Park and all that fine open country to live in?"

"Oh, well," said Cheapside, "don't let's 'ave that old argument all over again. 'Ere we are, comin' to the Park now. Most of the leaves is fallen. But it's nice any time of year."

As John Dolittle entered at the gates of Regent's Park he had to admit that this was indeed, as Mrs. Cheapside had said, an ideal place for a city sparrow to make his home. Big elms, horse chestnuts and all manner of other trees rose from the wide greenswards. Fine, well-kept flower beds bordered the walks. Snug, secluded shrubberies, fenced off from the public, offered safe and quiet nesting thickets. Nor was it by any means too countrified for a city-bred bird. Human company, from which the house sparrow seldom stays far away,was here in plenty. Nurse maids, pushing perambulators and leading children, were everywhere. And through this park all the visitors to the Zoological Gardens had to pass. There were open-air restaurants, where families out for the day could take their meals at little tables beneath the big elms. The plump, well-fed sparrows gobbling up the crumbs showed that no bird need starve in this part of London.

"Yes, Doctor," said Cheapside, when John Dolittle called his attention to this, "but for grub I'm still better off in the city proper. For good kitchen service the Café de Gutter 'as got this beaten easy."

"The Café de *what?*" asked the Doctor.

"The Café de Gutter," Cheapside repeated. "You know—the all-night coffee stall—lunch wagons. 'Ere in the park folks only 'old picnics in the summer. Cold, perishin' winter days, when a sparrer is really 'ard up for a bite, you can't get anything 'ere. Oh, when it's warm, yes, you could choke a helephant to death on all the 'ard-boiled heggs and sandwich scraps a' blossimin' on the lawns. But not in winter—hoh, no indeed! Folks don't come out lookin' at the pretty polar bears when there's an east wind blowin'. But the coffee stall, that's open all night. Cabbies, bobbies, street washers, market gardeners coming up to the counter regular every five minutes, dribblin' their crumbs down on to the pavement. I know this bloomin' city back to front, I do. And I says, to keep the wolf from the door—in all weathers, mind you—roost me next to the Café de Gutter."

"Well, you could live here in summer," said his wife, "and go back to the cathedral for the winter, couldn't you? That's what I've been asking you to do for the last three years and more. It's better for the children, too—to be brought up in this quiet, restful park, instead of goin' to sleep every night to the racket of the cab wheels and the yelling of the newspaper boys."

"That's all right, Becky," said Cheapside. "But, just the same, our youngsters 'ave all thriven on it. When some of 'em was peevish and wanted special dainty foods there wasn't nothing you'd mention that I couldn't get you at a moment's notice. You remember them hasparagus tips I pinched from the Covent Garden Market at four o'clock in the mornin', when Bertie was 'avin spasms in 'is stummick? Huh! Like to know where you'd get such dainties anywhere else in a hemergency. No, take it all round, Becky, you can't beat St. Paul's. It's so central."

CHAPTER TWO

CHEAPSIDE TELLS A STORY

Even before they reached the entrance to the Zoo inclosure John Dolittle was greeted by several animals that inhabited the park in a free, wild state. Portly wood pigeons flew down from the great elms, cooed good day and told him they were glad to see him in the city. Squirrels, full of cheeky energy, came bounding out from under rhododendron bushes and bade him welcome. For these creatures Cheapside, proud as Punch to be the great man's guide, showed the most utter contempt.

"All squirrels are thieves—natural pickpockets," he said. "And all wood pigeons are gluttons. When Becky and me lived here regular it took us all our time to get a decent meal when them fellers were around."

At the entrance to the Zoo the Doctor paid his admission at a little window.

"You don't 'ave to pay for us, Doc," chuckled Cheapside.

"We fly in over the top. And anyway we're entitled to season tickets because we used to be residents 'ere."

"You ought to be members of the Royal Zoological Society," laughed the Doctor.

"Well, I reckon we know as much natural 'istory as some members I could mention," said Cheapside.

Inside, the first thing the Doctor noticed was that some of the pens were being painted and many evidently just done.

"Oh, it's a good Zoo, this," said Cheapside, gazing round with pride. "They always keep it spic and span. The paint smells awful while it's drying. But this Zoo is the cleanest, best kept in the world."

In a big space near the bandstand there was a restaurant. And the Doctor thought that before starting on his tour of inspection he would like a cup of tea. So he sat down at one of the small tables and was presently served by a waitress. Becky and Cheapside shared the Doctor's meal (much to the envy of the other Zoo sparrows who gathered around) by standing beside his teacup and gobbling the cake crumbs that fell from the great man's plate.

"Over there," said Cheapside, "on t'other side of the bandstand you 'ave our prize exhibit."

"It looks to me like another tea garden," said the Doctor gazing across the clearing.

"That's what it is," said the sparrow. "It's the members' inclosure. See the sign: *'For members only.'* It's for members of the Royal Zoological Society. That's for fear you might think it was for members of the monkey 'ouse. That old scarecrow in the 'igh black 'at, that's Sir William Gigglebeak, F. R. Z. S. 'E knows less about natural 'istory than any man living. But 'e's always on show 'ere, drinking 'is tea in the members' inclosure. Did you ever see such a face? I wonder the children don't throw 'im peanuts. Look at 'im a' gazin' at us through 'is monocle, super-silly-ass like. 'E's

Squirrels came bounding out from under the bushes

wonderin' who you are, Doc. That's a joke, isn't it? 'Im what don't know one end of an animal from another, puttin' on airs with you, the greatest naturalist the world ever saw! Yes, that's a good one, that is."

"What is that large cage next door to the inclosure?" asked the Doctor, pouring out a second cup of tea.

"Oh, that's the Crested Screamers' Aviary," said Cheapside. "Good fellows, they are, Screamers. All birds like 'em. From time beyond recollection they've protected smaller birds from harm—when they was wild, that is. That's why I used to get currants for 'em when I lived 'ere. They love 'em."

"Currants?" said the Doctor. "Where did you get them?"

"I used to pick them out of the members' buns, said Cheapside, "over at the tea house next door. Yes, old William Gigglebeak 'ad to go without currants in 'is bun when I lived 'ere. They all went to the Screamers. It's funny, that saved my life once—doing them a good turn."

"How was that?" asked the Doctor.

"It's a long story," said Becky, gobbling a piece of bread which John Dolittle had given her.

"Well, I should like to hear it," said the Doctor. "What you tell me of the Screamers protecting all the other birds interests me. Go ahead, Cheapside. We have a long walk before us to get round the whole collection. And I'll be glad of another ten minutes' rest."

"Well," Cheapside began, "it was about a month after I came to live 'ere that the Crested Screamers were first brought to the Zoo. I remember their arrival well. There was considerable excitement in the bird collection all around, because, of course, we knew their reputation. And me, along with half a dozen other sparrows what made the Zoo their home, goes to call on the newcomers. They seemed kind of mopey and down-in-the-mouth, 'cause they'd only just been captured not so long ago. So we tried our best to make 'em feel they were among friends. And the first thing I asks 'em is what they like best in the food line. They wasn't very interested, to begin with. But presently, when a few of 'em had worked up an appetite, they admits that their greatest delicacy was currants, dried currants.

" 'All right,' I says, 'I'll have to see what can be done,' and off I flits on a sort of foragin' expedition. I goes to the ordinary restaurant and tea shops. Then I visits the old feller who keeps the sweetmeat stall—you know, sells chocolates and goodies for the children. But I don't find no currants—pretty much everything else in the food line, but no currants. So then Becky says to me, she says: ' 'Ow about the Members Inclosure? They 'ave tea there continual. Let's go and see if we can't get some currants there.'

"So we trundles off together to inspect the Members' menoo. Well, we was just disgusted. They kept nothing but seed cake. Seems old Gigglebeak was very partial to it. Then I puts on my thinking cap. And after considerin' heavy for a while I says to Becky, I says, 'We've got to fix it so they keep currant buns or currant cake in the Members' Tea House.'

" 'Yes,' she says, 'but 'ow are you goin' to manage it?'

" 'The rats,' I says. 'Let's go and see the rats.' "

CHAPTER THREE

CURRANTS FOR THE SCREAMERS

"Then we goes to the back door of the house kitchen and 'angs around there till an old rat comes chasing 'isself out of a hole next the cellar winder.

" 'Look 'ere,' I says, grabbin' 'im by the tail. 'I would 'ave words with you. Them Crested Screamers what came in last night is a special kind of bird what always protects smaller birds in the wild state. It's up to us to see that they're kept comfortable when they're down on their luck and in captivity, see? Now, they only keep seed cake 'ere for the Members. What we want you to do is to pinch the seed cake or spoil it in some way—you have the run of the larder and you know where it's kept, and all that—and continue pinchin' it or spoilin' it till they give up keeping seed cake and take currant buns, see?'

" 'Oh, no,' 'e says, wiggling 'is whiskers virtuous-like, 'I don't see 'ow I can do that.'

" 'Well,' I says, 'you jolly well find out a way—and quick. It's up to all us fellers that makes our home in the Zoo 'ere to see that the Screamers are treated right in return for what they've done for the smaller fellers when they was free. And if you don't fall in with my ideas I'll tell every bloomin' animal in the Zoo to treat you as a foreign henemy. You live on the scraps fed to the exhibits, same as what we do. Well, take my word for it, you'll 'ave a very thin time if you don't do as

I say. Now, get all your friends on the job and hop about it.'

"Them rats," Cheapside continued, "managed it all right. In fact they started out by doing it too well, you might say. What do you think they did? The oldest of 'em—oh, an artful old dodger, 'e was—the one I'd spoken to, 'e goes and spills a bottle of rat poison on the seed cake. 'E'd been at the game so long, dodging traps and ferrets and all the other inventions for killin' rats, that 'e knew the smell—even with a cold in 'is 'ead—of every rat poison on the market. And in all 'is cunnin' ways 'e 'ad instructed the other rats that lived under the tea house. Well, 'e knew where the bottle of poison was kept and after I left 'im 'e goes and spills it all over the seed cake what was set out in the pantry for to-morrow's tea."

Cheapside paused a moment, grinning thoughtfully.

"You never saw such an 'ow-d'ye-do," he chuckled presently. "That afternoon about four o'clock me and Becky 'ears a great commotion over at the Members' Inclosure. We 'ops across to see what it was all about, and there was Sir William Gigglebeak being carried off to 'ospital with a terrible pain in 'is stummick. You know, the funny part of it was that that particular rat poison was Sir William's hinvention—'is only contribution to the science of natural 'istory, in fact. And 'e was very proud of it. But 'is nose wasn't scientific enough to catch the smell of it on the seed cake. So I says to Becky, I says, ' 'E ought to rechristen 'is mixture *Members' Poison* and mark the poison *For Members Only* like the sign on the tea house.'

" 'But lor bless me! she says, 'this is serious, you know. We can't 'ave the Members killed off like this. You better go and see that rat again and tell 'im to think of something else.'

" 'All right,' I says. 'Though I don't fancy most of the Members would be any great loss to natural 'istory. Still, maybe you're right.'

"Sir William Gigglebeak carried off to hospital"

"So we goes round to the tea house kitchen and tells our friend 'is methods, while they was thorough, was a bit drastic, and 'e must find some other way to cure the Members' taste for seed cake. But as a matter of fact there wasn't no need for no further conspirin' on our part. Old William Gigglebeak got well again after about two weeks of colic; and when 'e showed up again at the Inclosure the first order 'e gave was that 'e didn't want to see no more seed cake in the tea house, never no more. Then they ordered in a lot of currant buns and plum cakes for the Members' tea; and we was all right. Me and Becky and a dozen of our pals used to spend two hours every afternoon picking up currants from under the chairs and even nicking them out of the buns on the tables when no one was lookin'. And we put our collection together every evening and took 'em across to the Crested Screamers and dribbled 'em in through the wire netting on the top of their cage."

CHAPTER FOUR

CHEAPSIDE HAS A NARROW ESCAPE

"Well, even though they was in captivity, the Screamers still did one small bird a good turn. And that was me. We 'ad a family of young ones in the nest and Becky 'ere used to ask me to go and get 'er suet every once in a while to feed 'em. You know young birds need a certain amount of meat. And sometimes I would get bits of fat out of the lions' den when they was sleeping after a heavy meal; and sometimes I'd get it other places. And among these places was the Owl House. In those days the Owl House stood next to the Screamers' Aviary, on the other side of the Members' Inclosure. It was a low shed, with the usual runway at the back, covered with wire nettin'; and it was divided into six compartments. In the center was the Great Horned Owl—an ugly old sinner if ever there was one! 'Our Mr. Grouch' we used to call 'im. Never had a good word to say to nobody.

"Our Mr. Grouch, the Great Horned Owl," Cheapside went on, "didn't like me poppin' into 'is cage for bits of meat—said so more than once and warned me to keep out of 'is territory if I didn't want me bloomin' 'ead bit off. But, as 'e usually slept on 'is perch most of the day, I used to slip through a tear in the netting and help meself without askin' 'is permission.

"One day Becky sent me out to get some suet, and after huntin' around several cages and pens without success I says to meself, I says, 'I'll go and try me luck in Mr. Owl's dinin' room.' And off I goes. Well, it was a fine afternoon and our Mr. Grouch was snoozin' on 'is perch, dead to the world. So I pops in through the rent in the nettin' and starts foragin' around quiet-like. I 'adn't been there more than a minute or two before a keeper comes in. And I slips behind the door, so I won't be seen. The keeper sweeps the place up a bit, and then, as luck would 'ave it, before he goes out he stands a heavy iron plate, what was used for the owl's meat, right over the hole in the nettin' what I'd been using as a door to get in and out by.

"Mr. Grouch had hardly woke up for the keeper's coming. And as soon as the coast was clear I starts hunting not for suet, but for a way to get out. The iron plate was much too heavy for me to move, so I searches the netting all over to see if I can find another hole to get through. I knew, of course, that, once Mr. Owl wakes, when the darkness comes it was all over with me. 'E'd warned me to keep out. And in the dark, against his eyes and quick flight, I wouldn't stand a chance. 'E'd just eat me. That was all there was to it. So you can bet I searched the nettin' pretty thorough. But not one blessed place could I find where a sparrow could get through.

" 'Well' I thought, 'my only 'ope is to 'ide somewhere till daylight. Then he'll go to sleep again and I may slip out when the keeper comes in with 'is breakfast.'

"So I tucks myself away in the corner behind 'is drinking bowl, says a prayer and 'opes for the best—wonderin' what Beck's thinking when I don't come back with the suet. Darkness begins to come on and Mr. Owl stretches 'isself and wakes up. The first thing he does is sniff!

" 'Oh Lord!' I thinks to meself. ' 'E smells me already!'

"And, sure enough, 'e starts right away 'unting around every corner of his place, just as though he knew for certain I was there. My fevvers stood straight up on the top of me 'ead with fright. At last 'e comes to the drinking bowl, peers behind it with those great eyes of 'is, glowin' like lamps in the dark, and see me!

" 'Now I've got you, you little devil!' 'e says. And he jumps for me. I shoots up into the air. And then a grand chase began all around the cage.

" 'It's no use,' I keeps sayin' to meself. ' 'E's bound to get me in the end. 'Is speed's twice as good as mine.'

"But I'd forgotten my friends, the Crested Screamers, next door. They'd seen me go into the Owl House, and they 'adn't seen me come out. And when they 'ears the two of us flutterin' around they guessed what was wrong. And suddenly the whole lot of 'em—a dozen there was—starts screaming at the top of their voices. And the watch-man thinkin' some animal has got loose, comes rushin' out with a lantern and goes all along the aviaries, to find out what the matter was. Then, seeing the Great Horned Owl a' thrashin' around the cage after something in the dark, he opens the door. And before you could say Jack Robinson I

" 'Now I've got you, you little devil!' "

was on the outside, lookin' in, makin' faces at Mr. Grouch and thankin' my lucky stars and the Crested Screamers."

"My gracious!" said the Doctor. "You had a narrow escape. But all's well that ends well."

"That's Shaker-spear—all's well wot ends well—ain't it, Doc?" asked Cheapside.

"Yes," laughed the Doctor. "Shakespeare said it first. It's a most useful quotation—fits a lot of situations. Shall we get on with the search?"

"Righto!" said the sparrow. "Come on Becky, let's show the Doctor the Owls. They'd make a roarin' good endin' for the first act of 'is opera. Sort of a *'Oo, 'Oo, 'OO's the Crew, Wot sails the Bloomin' Bloo,* chorus."

The Green Breasted Martins

CHAPTER ONE

THE LAND OF THE GAMBIA GOO-GOOS

MANY YEARS ago Doctor Dolittle went to Africa to cure the monkeys who were sick. The part of the country where he landed was called the Land of the Jolliginki and the King of the Jolliginki didn't like stangers in his lands. So he threw the Doctor and his family into jail. Prince Bumpo, the King's son, was kind-hearted and secretly let the Doctor and his animal family escape. They made a hasty departure from the land without carefully checking their provisions.

Poor Bumpo, who knew little about the needs of a sailing voyage—having lived on land all his life—had gone into the King's cellars and, in the dark, snatched any boxes that were near at hand and popped them into the Doctor's ship.

Dab-Dab, the duck, who was chief cook on the voyage, was horrified when she opened box after box and found nothing but yams—a sort of sweet potato.

"Yams! Yams!" she complained. "How can I prepare a decent meal with nothing but yams!"

"Heavens preserve us!" groaned Gub-Gub, the pig. "But I know that the King ate parsnips as well because I smelt them when those horrible soldiers were dragging us through the palace jail. That stupid Bumpo! Why didn't he look in the boxes? I'll starve before I'll eat this stuff!"

"Oh, be quiet!" snapped Dab-Dab. "You wouldn't starve if you didn't eat until you got home! There's enough fat on your ribs to feed you for a month!"

"Now, now, Dab-Dab," said the Doctor. "It's natural for pigs to be fat. How do you cook yams?"

"I wouldn't know!" said Dab-Dab in a huff.

"It's quite easy," said the pushmi-pullyu. "You peel the yams, cut them up and then fry them in the palm oil. That's what is called palm oil chop, the commonest dish of the black people. I'll show you how it's done."

"Thank you," said the Doctor. "It's lucky we had you with us—without somebody who knew African cooking we might have starved."

"What's this stuff?" asked Jip, the dog, who was undoing one of the other boxes. "It smells horrible!"

"Dried locusts," said the pushmi-pullyu. "They are a kind of large grasshopper. You fry them, too. They're quite good."

"Pooh! Insects!" snorted Jip.

Everybody was very hungry. And after the pushmi-pullyu had shown them in the ship's kitchen how to prepare palm oil chop they all tried it and were surprised to find that it was not half bad. The grasshoppers, however, of which there was a great quantity in the hold, they refused to touch.

But after a few days having the same dish for breakfast, lunch and supper began to get tiresome. Now, for the first part of the journey home the ship kept sailing along northward; still in sight of the coast of Africa. And one night, after super, when they were all feeling more than usually tired of palm oil chop, the Doctor said:

"I think it would be a good idea, as soon as we have got safely past the Kingdom of Jolliginki, if we stopped and went ashore some place and got a few bananas. I have no doubt that these yams are very nourishing, but I for one, am heartily sick of them."

"I think that would be a very good plan," said Gub-Gub.

The next day about ten o'clock in the morning they passed the mouth of a beautiful river.

"That looks like a good place to get bananas," said the Doctor. "I think we'll steer the boat in there and see."

So the ship's nose was turned toward the land, and presently they entered the mouth of a very lovely, wide stream. Passing up the river a few miles, between thickly wooded banks, they finally brought the ship to anchor close to a large town of straw huts.

This town happened to be the chief town of the Goo-Goo people—that is, the Gambia Goo-Goos—whose country stretched for some miles inland from this point.

The Doctor remarked at once that it was a much pleasanter country than the one they had left, and the town bigger and better built than that of the Jolliginki.

The swallows which were flying along over the Doctor's ship turned also when they saw the boat change its course, and, entering the river, they settled down upon the banks around the ship, causing great astonishment to the Goo-Goo people. The townsfolk were not accustomed to have many boats visit their harbour, but to have one come accompanied by a great flock of birds, was, of course, something they had never seen before.

Stepping ashore, the Doctor was greeted by the Chief of the Goo-Goos, who asked him very politely if there was anything he could do for him. The Doctor made the Chief a present of an extra pocketknife he had, and then explained that he needed provisions for his ship and that he had come into this port expecting to find at least some fruit.

The Chief of the Goo-Goos asked him what foodstuffs, besides fruit, he would like. And Gub-Gub smacked his lips while the Doctor reeled off a long list of eatables.

"I am not sure," said the Chief, "that I shall be able to get you all these, but I will get you as many as I can."

He then gave orders to several servants and messengers who stood about him in attendance. And before long the Doctor and his animals saw a long line of porters going down to the ship with loads of food upon their heads.

"How wonderfully simple!" said the Doctor, watching them. "Now, if I had stopped at Liverpool to have the ship provisioned it would have taken me a week to get that done."

CHAPTER TWO

THE DOCTOR'S PLAN

John Dolittle then thanked the Chief many times and asked him if there was anything he could do for him in return. But the Chief, who seemed no end pleased with his new pocketknife, told him that no return or thanks were necessary—it was a pleasure, he said, and he hoped the Doctor would call again.

Returning to the river bank, John Dolittle saw that some great commotion was going on among the swallows. They had been joined by a number of green-breasted birds with whom they were now chattering and jabbering away in a very excited and agitated manner.

Now, it happened that this town of the Goo-Goos had been visited some months before by a white lady. She wrote books; she had short hair; she wore a collar and tie. She was, in fact, the kind of lady that was called in England in those days the New Woman. As soon as she set foot in Goo-Goo Land she had started bossing the Chief around, telling him how to run his country, how to bring up his children and a whole lot of other things which she thought he ought to know.

The Chief had not liked her very much and was heartily glad to see her go home again. But the Goo-Goo wives had admired the New Woman tremendously. They had never seen husbands and chiefs bossed about before by women, having been all their own lives very obedient to their menfolk—as is the custom in Africa. They could not understand how the white woman worked this "charm"—for magic of some kind, they thought, was the only thing that could give a woman such powers.

At last they decided that it must be in the strange hat she wore upon her head. This was a man's felt hat with a bird's wing on it—the wing of a green-breasted martin. So wanting to be like the new woman who bossed men around, all the Goo-Goo wives had to have a felt hat with a martin's wing on it. With that, they thought, they would surely be able to boss their husbands all they wanted.

This New Woman idea spread all over the Goo-Goo country. And although the Chief, terrified at the thought of having thousands of women in his land like the English writer of books, gave orders that it should stop, the New Women still met and worked in secret. And the poor martins were trapped and shot in great quantities to provide wings for felt hats.

Now, the martins—this particular kind was the green-breasted martin—are first cousins to the swallows. And they were now telling their troubles to those swallows who were traveling with the Doctor. This was what all the commotion was about which John Dolittle saw as he came back to his ship in the river.

When the Doctor got close to his ship six of the swallows who were leaders came to him and complained of the treatment that their cousins, the green-breasted martins, had suffered from the Goo-Goo bird hunters.

If something isn't done about this soon," said the swallows, "the martins in this country will be wiped right out. It's a perfect shame."

"But couldn't they go somewhere else?" asked the Doctor, "to some other land where they wouldn't be hunted for hats?"

"At any other time they could," said the swallows. "But this is the nesting season for them. And the eggs and young birds cannot be left to get cold."

"Humph! What do these martins live on?" asked the Doctor.

"Flies—the same as we do," said the swallows. "Mosquitoes and small moths are their favourite food. But they will eat any kind of flying insects. Now, in this country many of the mother birds whose husbands have been killed are dying of cramps, sitting on the nests afraid to leave to get food, and with no mates to bring it to them."

"Dear me! This is a terrible thing," said the Doctor. "Terrible! I'll go back and speak to the Chief about it."

So the Doctor went and asked the Chief of the Goo-Goos

if he could not do something to stop the killing of these beautiful birds.

The Chief said he would do what he could and at once sent messengers throughout the whole of the Goo-Goo country with orders that the killing of martins must stop.

Then John Dolittle came back to his ship and sent word to the martins of what he had done. The martins thanked him, but asked that he remain here a few days to see if the orders were carried out.

So for some days the Doctor's ship stayed in the river, after it had been moved a little further from the town to a better anchorage. And John Dolittle now had time to travel up the stream by canoe to explore and see the country.

When he got back the martins came to him again, saying that the Chief's orders were not being obeyed, that two hundred more birds had been killed secretly and put on felt hats since he left.

For a moment the Doctor was silent, frowning with furious indignation. Then he asked that all the leaders of both the martins and the swallows meet him in the cabin of his ship right away to discuss the situation.

"Now, tell me," said John Dolittle as soon as they had all found comfortable places around the big table to perch on, "you martins live on flies, mosquitoes and moths, do you not?"

"Yes," said the martins, "but only on the smaller moths; the big fuzzy ones give the young birds hiccups. We like mosquitoes best—for summer diet there's nothing like a good, juicy mosquito."

"Fine!" said the Doctor. "Now, my idea is this: Mosquitoes sting people, you know—most uncomfortable. And moths eat clothes. And a lot of other insects, like flying ants and beetles, would be a fearful nuisance to people, if you birds did not keep them down by eating them. What I propose is that you should stop eating flies and insects for a while. They will then become a great pest. Then perhaps I'll be able to persuade the Goo-Goo wives to obey the Chief's orders and leave you alone."

"But what are we to live on in the meantime?" asked the martins. "We're not like finches and starlings; you know we must have insect food."

"Ah!" said the Doctor. "I hadn't thought of that."

Then Gub-Gub, who with the other animals was listening intently (since the conversation was about food), said:

"Doctor, I have an idea."

"Splendid!" said John Dolittle. "What is it, Gub-Gub?"

"Downstairs in the hold of this ship," said the pig, "there are fifty packing cases full of dried locusts. Why can't the martins live on them while you are bringing the Goo-Goo wives to their senses?"

"Excellent!" cried the Doctor. "Do you think," he asked, turning to the martins, "that you could feed your babies on dried locusts for a while?"

"Oh, certainly," said the martins—"if we had to."

"All right," said the Doctor. "Now, listen: We must make a thorough job of this. I want you leaders to send out messengers to all the fly-catchers and insect-eaters in this district—martins, swallows, swifts, whippoorwills, shrikes, every kind. Tell them that dried locusts in plenty will be set out on the deck of this ship for them to come and eat and take to their young ones. But no live insect must be touched from now on till I give the word. Understand? And if we can't persuade the Goo-Goo ladies to change the style in hats within a very short space of time I shall be greatly surprised. The conference is over. Now, send out your messengers and keep me informed of how things are going."

By nightfall the leaders returned to the Doctor and told him that his orders had been carried out. All the insect-eating birds (of which there are a great number of different kinds in Africa, a fine hunting ground for bugs) had willingly agreed to help by leaving all moths, mosquitoes and ants strictly alone.

CHAPTER THREE

SPEEDY—THE SKIMMER

And for the next two weeks the scene around the Doctor's boat was very gay, with myriads of brightly coloured flycatchers of all kinds coming and going to feed on the dried locusts set out for them on the deck.

At the end of twenty days the results of the Doctor's plan were quite surprising—even to John Dolittle himself. For, you see, all the insects, now being left strictly alone by the birds, began to lay thousands and thousands of eggs and to have huge, big families, and to multiply and increase in the most alarming way.

The first sign of success that came to those on the ship was when Gub-Gub woke up in the middle of the night, crying out that he was all over mosquito bites. One by one the rest of the ship's company were awakened and kept awake by the stinging flies.

"Ah, hah!" said the Doctor, sitting up in bed and busily

swatting in all directions. "This is splendid. I wonder how the Goo-Goo ladies like this."

But the mosquito plague grew and grew—more terrible every hour. Those on the ship really suffered a great deal for the sake of their friends, the martins. When the Doctor and the animals ventured on deck in the morning they found the air outside thick with mosquitoes and flying ants, and they were finally driven back by the pests into their cabin again. Then they slammed the doors shut and stuffed up every crack to keep out the swarming insects.

Poor Gub-Gub was a dreadful sight—he was, in fact, nothing but one large pink mosquito bite. The Doctor had to put him to soak in a bathtub of boracic acid to reduce the swelling. And as for the pushmi-pullyu, having no tail to use as a fly swat, he had a perfectly terrible time. But he never grumbled.

Of course, they could not very well stay shut up in the cabin without any fresh air for days on end, and soon the Doctor realized that he must get some protection from the flies for himself and his animals. So he sent for one of the swallow leaders.

In answer to his summons it was the chief of the leaders that came, a very neat, trim little bird, with long, long wings and sharp, snappy eyes. Speedy-the-Skimmer he was called, a name truly famous throughout the whole of the feather world. He was the champion fly-catcher of Africa, Europe and America. For years every summer he had won all the flying races, having broken his own record only last year by crossing the Atlantic in eleven and a half hours at a speed of more than two hundred miles an hour.

"Speedy," said the Doctor. "I and my party are imprisoned in our ship here. We dare not go out to take the air or stretch our legs for fear of the mosquitoes and biting flies. Can you do anything for us?"

"Why, certainly," said Speedy. "I'll tell off a few hundred

Speedy-the-Skimmer he was called

wrens to mount guard over the ship here and keep the mosquitoes away from you and your party. They'll take care of you. Your scheme is working splendidly, Doctor. The Goo-Goo ladies are having a frightful time. They're much worse off than you are, you know, because they wear fewer clothes and the flies have more room to bite. I'll send you the wrens right away."

So saying, Speedy flew off. And from that time on the Doctor's ship had a special guard of nine hundred wrens—very small birds, but marvelous fly-catchers. John Dolittle and his pets were now able to come safely out on deck and take the air and enjoy themselves.

Two days after that, in the morning before it was quite daylight, the Doctor said to Jip:

"I think I ought to go ashore into the town to see what's going on. I notice that the ants and beetles have started increasing at a great pace the last day or so. I am a little bit uneasy. I mustn't let this thing go too far."

From the deck the animals watched the Doctor depart. For protection he had gloves on his hands, and his head, all but the eyes, was covered with a red handkerchief.

"I'm glad he didn't take any of us with him," said Gub-Gub, who was now entirely recovered from his bites. "Just look at the flies swarming around his head!"

It was not long after John Dolittle left that Too-Too, the owl, suddenly cried:

"Oh, look! Here comes the Doctor back, running. Goodness, he's all excited—waving his arms! See! I wonder what has happened in the town."

Dab-Dab, Gub-Gub, Jip, Too-Too, the pushmi-pullyu, and the white mouse crowded to the rail of the ship as the Doctor came bounding down to the river.

"What is it, Doctor," called the owl as soon as the Doctor was within earshot—"flies?"

"No," gasped the Doctor, as he came panting up on the deck. "Ants!—flying ants, black ants, red ants, white ants

—ants in hundreds and thousands and millions. You can't see the houses any more—nothing but mounds and mounds of ants."

"What has happened to the people?" asked Dab-Dab.

"They've shut themselves inside the houses. But the ants are eating the houses up—they're only made of grass. It's what they'll do when they've eaten the houses that I'm afraid of. Heaven help the people if the ants are still hungry then! Too-Too, get the Skimmer for me as quick as you can. Hurry, or the whole of Goo-Goo Land will be wiped out!"

CHAPTER FOUR

THE MARTINS ARE SAVED

So off went Too-Too to find Speedy.

"My gracious! I had no idea matters had gone so far as this," said the Doctor, sitting down and mopping his brow. "It's lucky I went to-day to take a look at the town. I kind of thought that something was wrong. . . . I do wish Too-Too would hurry. There isn't a moment to lose. Ah, good! Here he is—and the Skimmer, too."

"Speedy," said the Doctor as soon as the trim little bird had settled on the deck. "The town of the Goo-Goos is being eaten up by ants. Tell all the fly-catchers to go back to work. Take them up yourself to the town and clear those ants away. Hurry, for pity's sake! It's the biggest job you ever had to do. You'll need every fly-catcher you can raise. And hurry, Speedy, as fast as you know how."

Then the swift and famous Skimmer rose high in the air on his curved and flashing wings of blue. And reaching to terrific height, he began letting out shriek after shriek—a high, piercing whistling cry. Those on the deck of the ship below watched him as he swept the sky in dizzy circles, calling, calling, calling: "Tee-wee-hee! Tee-wee-hee! Tee-wee-HEE!"

And very soon, in answer to the swallow leader's cry, fly-catchers of every description, colour and kind left whatever they were doing and came swirling into the air in a dark and ever growing mass above the Doctor's ship.

Then suddenly, led by Speedy-the-Skimmer, the enormous army of birds made off for the town at a terrific pace. The rush of those millions of wings through the air was like the North Wind gone mad.

"Come along," said the Doctor. "We must see that the Goo-Goos are rescued from their plight. I started this—I've got to see it through."

The animals all jumped up and followed him as he left the ship and raced off toward the town.

As they drew near to it a curious buzzing noise reached their ears. Tremendous—like some great machine purring, whirring smoothly—it grew and grew; the noise of millions and millions of insects working busily in the sun.

When the animals got closer the sight that met their eyes was indeed a strange one. You couldn't see the houses of the town at all. Over everything in view lay a thick moving carpet of ants.

"Golly!" said Too-Too. "I'm glad I'm not a Goo-Goo. How on earth are they ever going to get out from under that mess?"

But even while he spoke the fly-catchers swept down

upon the moving carpet in countless numbers. And then began the most terrific battle ever seen by mortal eyes.

It lasted three hours. And, although the fly-catchers won, by the time the last of the ants and beetles and moths and mosquitoes had been driven away, the birds were so exhausted that they sat and lay and squatted in panting, weary millions on the ground, hardly able to move their wings another flip.

And now could be seen what work of havoc the insects had done. The straw thatching of the huts was all eaten away; only the bare poles remaining. The shade trees before the doors were stripped of their leaves, bare, as though winter had come in a night. And from within the frames of the dwellings frightened, huddled families of black folk gazed out at the white man and the millions of birds who had saved them from destruction. Not a rag of clothing remained among the lot of them, for the moths had eaten every scrap of wool and cotton they possessed; not a vestige of a roof remained above their heads, and they themselves were covered with mosquito bites. But their lives were saved. The Doctor and Speedy-the-Skimmer had arrived only just in time.

In a little while the Goo-Goos came timidly out of the wrecks of their homes, and then John Dolittle made a speech to them.

"People of Goo-Goo Land," said he, "you have to-day been rescued from a great and terrible danger. And it was these little green birds you see about you here that saved you—the same birds that, in spite of your Chief's orders, you shot and trapped to make hats out of. They came to me on my arrival in your land and complained. And, seeing no other way would bring you to your senses, I told them to stop doing the useful work which they do for you all their lives. That work is the eating of flies and insects. I hoped when you should see what happens when that work is

Huddled families gazed out at the white man

stopped that you would realize how foolish you have been in killing them. Do you realize it now?"

Then all the wives who had wanted to be New Women rose up and shouted:

"We do, we do!"

"I am glad of that," said the Doctor. "Do you promise that the Green-breasted Martin shall for all time be safe and unharmed in your land?"

"A sacred bird in Goo-Goo Land forever!"

"We do, we do!" shouted the Goo-Goos. "The Green-breasted Martins who saved our lives this day shall be a sacred bird in Goo-Goo Land forever! Woe to any one who touches a feather of the Sacred Martin! May the Fifty-nine Curses of Hullagoozelum fall upon his head!"

Then the Chief, in a deep, bass voice, began reciting the Fifty-nine dread Curses of Hullagoozelum for the benefit of any one who should henceforth molest a martin:

"May his hammock strings break in the dead of night, letting him fall into the deepest mud. May he, when he rests beneath the palm at noon, have hard and knobby cocoanuts descend upon his head. May he"—

"That will do, please," the Doctor interrupted. "You can recite the rest of the Fifty-nine after I'm gone. I see that many of your community have been severely bitten by the flies. If those of you who wish for medical treatment will come down to my ship your injuries will be attended to."

Then the Doctor and his animals moved off toward the river. And all the Goo-Goos followed him, murmuring to one another:

"Truly he must be a great man whom the very birds obey —greater by far than the white woman who was insolent to chiefs, a disturber of the peace and a fake magician, leading us astray."

And now for many hours John Dolittle, M. D., was kept more than busy attending to fly-bitten Goo-Goos. His supply of witch hazel, bay rum, boracic acid, ammonia and bicarbonate of soda soon ran out. And he had to get herbs from the jungle and boil them down and make more lotions for his many patients.

It was halfway through the night before he was done, and he was very weary. But the Goo-Goos, after his treatment, were feeling fit as fiddles. The Doctor then set to helping them rebuild their homes. These being of straw, were quickly repaired.

Then a feast was made ready by the Chief's wives in honour of the Doctor, and everybody sat down, and there was much laughter and merriment.

The next morning the Goo-Goos provisioned the Doctor's ship with proper foods for the balance of the journey. There was bacon and flour, prunes and cocoa for the Doctor, parsnips and cabbages for Gub-Gub, and plenty of tea and sugar for everyone. They even remembered to include some bones for Jip and seeds for Too-Too and the white mouse. When they finally brought aboard two bales of hay for the pushmi-pullyu the hold was full to the hatches.

"Good-bye, good-bye!" cried the Goo-Goos as the ship slowly moved away from the harbor. "Safe journey home!"

The Lost Boy

CHAPTER ONE

LONDON ZOO

DOCTOR DOLITTLE, Cheapside, the London Sparrow, and Becky, the sparrow's wife were in the Zoological Gardens looking for birds of all sorts to sing in the Doctor's Canary Opera. On the way to the bird enclosure they came upon many signs which read: *"Lost Children Will Be Taken To The Ladies' Cloak Room."*

"Yes," said Cheapside, noticing the Doctor reading this sign for the third time. "That's so the mothers and fathers and uncles will know where to look for their nippers when they get lost. Folks is awful careless. On Saturdays and Sundays the Ladies' Cloak Room is just full of little lost Willies and Aggies. I always used to say they ought to learn 'em tricks and put 'em in a pen alongside the monkeys."

Shortly after this, as the Doctor was passing one of the ponds for waterfowl, he noticed a small red-headed boy trying to wade out to feed the ducks. Fearing he might tumble in, the Doctor leaped over a low railing and grabbed the child by its pinafore. Then he looked around to find the youngster's mother or guardian. But no one at all seemed to be with him. The Doctor questioned him, but all the boy would answer was:

"I want to feed the ducks."

"Take him to the Ladies' Cloak Room, Doctor," said Cheapside. "Don't argue with him. He's lost, all right. Come along. I'll show you the way."

The Doctor grabbed the child by its pinafore

So, with the Doctor leading the little fellow by the hand, they set off along a winding path through shrubberies.

At the cloak room the woman in charge took the child and thanked the Doctor for bringing him.

"This is the second time he's been brought back to-day, sir," said she. "I've no idea who owns him. No one has put in a claim."

"I don't wonder at that," whispered Cheapside to Becky at the door. " 'E's no beauty. I wouldn't be surprised if they lost 'im on purpose."

"Sh!" said Becky. "Maybe 'e's heir to a throne or something. I've heard tell how princes was lost deliberate by wicked uncles and things."

"Heir to a kitchen chair!" snorted Cheapside with disdain. " 'E ain't no prince. Princes don't 'ave 'air that colour."

The boy seemed to have taken a liking to the Doctor. For when he was left in the woman's charge he bawled heartily at John Dolittle's departure. And about half an hour later, when the Doctor was busy conversing with the birds in the East Aviary, he suddenly found the red-headed child once more standing beside him.

" 'E's escaped from the cloak room again," said Cheapside in disgust. "Better tell the woman this time to lock 'im in the cupboard—or maybe we'll be arrested for kidnapin' before the day's over."

Once more the Doctor returned the lost one to the care of the woman in charge of the cloak room. And this time he gave her special instructions to guard him carefully till his parents came for him.

"Dear me!" said John Dolittle, as he hurried back to the aviary. "This has wasted quite a little of our time. I wonder who he is—look, it is beginning to get dark. We had better abandon our search for to-day."

In spite of the lateness of the hour and the growing darkness, Mr. and Mrs. Cheapside insisted on seeing the Doctor home. And together they left the Zoological Gardens and set out for Greenheath.

"I'll probably decide on pelicans for the bassos and flamingoes for baritones," said the Doctor. "The higher voices we can do with linnets and such like, which we will get from the fields. Do you think you would be able to get me some pelicans and flamingoes, Cheapside?" the Doctor asked as they made their way through Regent's Park.

"Well, maybe," said the sparrow. "I know of one place about ten miles from the city where a rich feller has a whole lot of fancy waterfowl—pelicans among them. How many would you want?"

"About six, I should think," said the Doctor, "and six flamingoes, too. But eight or ten would make a better chorus."

"Yes, that would be enough to sing any one to sleep—for good—I should say," murmured the sparrow. "Maybe there's that many at this feller's place. I'll take a run over there in the morning and let you know. I ain't sure about the flamingoes. Maybe I'll have to go elsewhere for them. You wouldn't want to buy them, would you?"

"Not if the gentleman will lend them to me," said the Doctor. "You see, the—what's that white, shadowy thing over there, hopping about among the trees?"

"What—where do you mean, Doctor?" asked Cheapside, peering through the trunks of the dim-lit park.

"Funny! It's gone now," said the Doctor. "I could have sworn I saw something pop behind that elm over there, the other side of the beds. Perhaps it was my imagination."

"Maybe some animal's got out from the menagerie—a deer or something." said Becky. "If it is, good luck to him, I say. I'd hate to live in captivity."

"Yes," said the Doctor. "I dislike the idea myself of

animals being confined against their will. In my private Zoo in Puddleby the cages all had locks on the *inside,* so the animals could get out when they wanted or shut themselves up at night, just for the sake of privacy, you know. But, oddly enough, although they were all free to go when they chose, none of them ever ran away."

"Yes," said Cheapside, "but yours was a real Zoo, Doc—run on proper lines. You always had a waiting list of animals to get *in,* instead of out. Goodness, don't I remember that old sleepy black bear you had who could never wake 'isself up in time for breakfast! You ought to 'ave seen that Zoo, Becky. Beat anything we saw on the Continent. Old Mr. Bear asked the Doctor for an alarm clock. And every night when he locked his own door, to keep out the tramps and the rats, you'd 'ear 'im a-windin' that old tin time-piece of 'is. O' course, 'e couldn't tell the time—used to look at the back, instead of the face, pretendin' 'e knew 'ow. But 'e knew enough to get up in time for breakfast when it went off in the mornin'! Ah, that was a real Zoo, that was—bless me! What's that runnin' be'ind us? Didn't you 'ear footsteps?"

CHAPTER TWO

JOHN DOLITTLE BRINGS HOME A GUEST

They were now come to the edge of Greenheath. And the wide open common, dotted with gorse clumps, stretched before them in the dim starlight. The three of them paused, listening.

"Hark to me, Cheapside," whispered Becky. "I believe there's something following us. Let the Doctor go on ahead and you and I hang back and do a little scouting. I think I 'eard something moving the other side of those bushes over there."

So the Doctor went on his way across the common of Greenheath while Mr. and Mrs. Cheapside hung back. And, keeping near the ground, where they would not be seen in the dim light, they set to work to find out who or what it was that was following them.

John Dolittle had pretty nearly made up his mind that it must be some animal, possibly escaped from the Zoo, that was determined to attach itself to his household. He had experienced this before many times. So great was his reputation among animals of every sort that he was constantly followed by lame dogs, rabbits, moles—all sorts of beasts who wished to consult him medically or see if they could be taken into his private circle of pets. But, the Doctor argued with himself, if it was nothing more than that why did the creature not come forward to see him, instead of slinking around like this in concealment?

As he walked forward over the springy turf of the heath

He could see the outline of his own circus tents

John Dolittle expected the sparrows any minute to overtake him with news. But, a good quarter of an hour passed without his hearing anything. And he could see the outline of his own circus tents not more than a few hundred yards away before Cheapside alighted on his shoulder and giggled:

"What d'yer think, Doctor? It's our red-headed friend, the nipper who was lost in the Zoo."

"Good heavens!" cried John Dolittle, stopping short. "The boy we left in the cloak room?"

"The very same, Doctor," said Cheapside. "If I was you I'd turn around and go back through the city some other way. That's about your only way of losing 'im."

"But, my gracious, Cheapside, I can't do that!" said the Doctor. "The child's lost. I can't leave him to wander around in the night like this. Where would he get supper? Where would he sleep?"

"Good lord, Doc!" said the sparrow impatiently. "That ain't your concern. What are you goin' to do, adopt 'im?"

"Well, I certainly can't leave him out here," said the Doctor. "Where is he? I'll have a talk with him."

So Cheapside guided the Doctor back a few yards to where Becky was keeping an eye on the boy behind a clump of gorse.

"Hulloa, my friend," said John Dolittle in a kindly voice. "Didn't your parents come for you at the Ladies' Cloak Room?"

"No," said the boy.

"But how did you come to be lost at the Zoo?"

"I wasn't lost by my parents," said the boy. "It was I who lost my parents. I want to be a menagerie keeper. So I ran away from home and came to the Zoo. But they would keep taking me to the Ladies' Cloak Room and saying I was lost. Then when it began to get dark and I saw they were going to close up the place I thought I'd follow you."

"Why?" asked the Doctor.

"Because I like you," said the boy.

"But what of your mother and father?" asked the Doctor.

"Oh, they're all right," said the boy. "They've got lots more children. I set out to seek my fortune—I want to be a menagerie keeper."

The Doctor took out his watch and peered at it in the dim light of the stars.

"Humph!" he muttered. "There's nothing else for it. You had better come and spend the night with me. And to-morrow I must try to get in touch with your parents."

"Who's that?" asked Gub-Gub as the Doctor entered his wagon leading the red-headed youngster by the hand.

"This is a young man who followed me all the way from the Zoo," said the Doctor, as the animals all gathered about him examining the small stranger. "He will spend the night with us. But I must get busy in the morning and find out who his parents are. Otherwise I may get arrested for kidnaping."

"For catnipping, did you say?" asked Gub-Gub, the pig.

"No. For kidnaping," the Doctor repeated—"that is, for stealing him. Some people might not believe that he followed me so far. Have you got some extra sheets, Dab-Dab?"

"Oh, I suppose I can find him a shakedown somewhere," said the housekeeper, wagging her tail in a harassed manner. "Tut! tut! I wonder you wouldn't have more sense, John Dolittle, than bringing him here when you know the wagon is so crowded already."

"But I didn't bring him," said the Doctor. "He followed me, I tell you I couldn't leave him out on the heath, with no blankets or anything."

"Well, anybody else would have found some other way out of the difficulty," snorted the duck. "It's bad enough to have you bringing in stray animals of every kind. But children! You don't realize what you've let yourself in for. Children make a terrible mess of a home. Gub-Gub will have to give up his bed and sleep on the floor."

"Who's that?" Gub-Gub asked

"Oh, goodness!" groaned the pig. "What with dieting for the opera and sleeping on the floor, I might as well be"—

At this point Matthew Mugg entered the wagon. In a few words the Doctor told him about the boy and the necessity for putting him up.

"Why don't you let him sleep in the menagerie, Doctor?" said Matthew. "There's two or three empty stalls there, with lots of clean straw."

"Did you say a menagerie?" asked the boy, his large round eyes showing intense interest. "What is this place?"

"This is a circus," said the Doctor—"the Dolittle Circus. And I am John Dolittle, the manager."

"A circus!" cried the youngster, stepping on Gub-Gub's tail in his excitement. "But how splendid! I set out to seek my fortune and I've found it. It's just like Dick Whittington. I wanted to be a keeper in the Zoo. I thought you must be something interesting when I saw you talking to the birds, like St. Francis. Of course, I'll sleep in the menagerie. I'll sleep with the elephant."

The boy, in spite of his being clearly tired from his long walk, was now all agog with the interest of his new position. He asked a thousand questions at once. And when supper was brought on he was so absorbed by the animals sitting around the table like people that he hardly ate anything. John Dolittle did his best to dissuade him from sleeping in the menagerie. But he was absolutely determined to spend the night with the elephant. And finally the Doctor had to carry him over there, almost too sleepy to keep his eyes open, and put him to bed under a pile of blankets. Alongside of the enormous animal he looked like a grasshopper next to a horse.

"Now, for heaven's sake," said the Doctor to the elephant, "don't roll in your sleep. If necessary, stay awake. It will only be for one night. To-morrow I hope to get this young man back to his parents."

CHAPTER THREE

TROUBLE AT THE CIRCUS

After spending a sleepless night himself, wondering whether the elephant had rolled on the child, the Doctor sped across to the menagerie almost before it was daylight. There he found the would-be keeper busily washing the elephant's face with a flannel. The enormous creature, realizing that the young tyrant meant well, was bearing the performance with patience while the boy walked about over his face, scrubbing it vigorously.

"I wish you'd take him away and let me get some rest," said the elephant miserably in answer to the Doctor's "Good morning." "I've hardly had a wink of sleep all night. I was so scared by what you said. When I did doze off I kept dreaming that I had squashed him out as flat as a pancake. And the first thing he did when he awoke—before I had a chance to get up—was to find a cake of soap and a floor rag and start cleaning my ears. I hardly slept a wink."

"Neither did I," said the Doctor.

The boy had now got hold of the menagerie broom and was busy brushing the elephant's hair with it.

"Er—pardon me," said John Dolittle, taking it from him. "But large animals don't have to have their hair brushed or their faces washed in the morning. They make their own toilet. How would it be if we went across to my wagon and had some breakfast?"

After a good deal of coaxing the young adventurer was taken off—much to the poor elephant's relief—to the manager's van.

. . . busily washing the elephant's face with a flannel

The first thing that Gub-Gub said when they entered the wagon was:

"Doctor, I didn't sleep a wink all night. I shall have to go to bed immediately after breakfast."

"Yes, and he kept me awake, too," growled Jip, the dog—"groaning and scratching the floor with his feet to make it soft!"

"Humph!" said the Doctor. "But you were not the only ones who did not sleep. Well, let's have breakfast, then maybe, we'll all feel better."

"I told you you were in for something, Doctor," said Dab-Dab as she set the porridge on the table. "Children are a handful. One child is more nuisance than a dozen animals."

"Yes, perhaps you're right, Dab-Dab," said the Doctor, sitting down. "I wonder why that is. Are you ever sorry you weren't born a man, Jip?"

"Good lord, no, Doctor!" said Jip. "I wouldn't be a man for anything."

"Why?" asked the Doctor, reaching for the cream.

"Men—people—worry such a lot," said Jip. "Their life is so—er—so complicated, difficult. Dogs never worry unless they're hungry or cold—or when they've lost their friends. Oh, no, I'm glad I wasn't born a man."

"That's rather curious, you know," said John Dolittle. "There have been philosophers who say that people are born over again—that some men have been animals and some animals men. It's called the theory of reincarnation."

"Then I bet Gub-Gub was a cook last time he was on earth," said Jip.

"Well, you can be sure I was a good cook, then, anyhow," said Gub-Gub indignantly. "I'll bet you I never served up anything as poor as this diet gruel. Gee, I'll be glad when that opera's over! This training is ruining my disposition."

The small red-haired adventurer apparently was highly pleased with his new home and had no intention of ever leaving it. All day long he insisted on helping with various parts of the show. He succeeded in getting in everybody's way to such an extent that it seemed that if something wasn't done about him soon there would be a general strike in the Dolittle Circus.

During the main performance in the big tent his determined efforts to take part in the show nearly cost him his life, when the lion stumbled during a balancing act and sat on him heavily. And the Doctor soon realized that Dab-Dab had been quite right and that one child could make more trouble than a dozen animals.

Seeing that it was urgently necessary to get him back to his home as soon as possible, the Doctor made a special trip into the city and put an advertisement in all the papers that a lost child with red hair could be claimed at his establishment on Greenheath. Meanwhile, the youngster, realizing the dream of his life, continued to have a wonderful time and to make himself what he thought was useful. He went into the clown's dressing room when no one was looking and daubed grease paint all over his face and pinafore. He called on the snakes during their performance and upset the tent and brought it down on top of the audience that was gathered there. He inspected the pushmi-pullyu, the two-headed animal, and made that poor, patient animal give him a ride on his back. He went to the performing otters' tent and fell in their tank and nearly drowned before they fished him out.

By nightfall, when the Doctor and Matthew were reduced to a state of complete exhaustion, keeping him out of harm and mischief, the young adventurer announced that he intended to sleep with the elephant again to-night. And in spite of that poor animal's begging to be allowed to get a good night's rest undisturbed—and the Doctor's trying for half an hour to dissuade the boy from his intention—he finally went to bed with his big friend, much to the relief of everyone except the elephant.

He daubed grease paint all over his face

"I don't know what I'll do," said the Doctor to Dab-Dab after supper, "if his parents don't come for him to-morrow. Advertising in the paper is about the only hope we have. I had expected that they'd be here to-day."

"It's your own fault," said Dab-Dab, "for bringing him here. You should have taken him to the police station."

"That's an idea," cried the Doctor. "Why didn't I think of that? Oh, but he wouldn't like it. He is having an awfully good time here."

"And what about the time we're having?" asked Dab-Dab. "You'll have that poor elephant sick again if you don't get that little imp out of here—and you know what a handful he is when he's sick. I saw him just break down and weep when he heard that the child was going to sleep with him again to-night. Take the little nuisance to the police station. They'll be kind to him—and they'll find his parents a lot quicker than you can."

"Humph!" murmured the Doctor. "I suppose there's something in what you say. Well, if his parents don't come in the morning I'll take him over there."

No one showed up the next day to claim the boy and Dab-Dab kept at the Doctor till she made him do as he had said he would. And about noon John Dolittle set out with the young man and left him in care of the local superintendent of police.

Everyone in the circus, especially the poor elephant, was greatly relieved to learn that he had gone, and the whole staff, which had been on the verge of open riot for two days, settled down once more to a peaceful life.

All that night again the Doctor hardly slept. This time his worry was not that the elephant might roll upon the boy, but how the youngster was getting on at the police station.

"You know, Dab-Dab," he said at breakfast next morning, "it seems such an inhospitable thing to do. The lad was having such a wonderful time here. And although I know, of course, that the police will treat him nicely, children are so funny, you understand. I couldn't help admiring the youngster—such pluck and determination—following me all that way from Regent's Park. And then for me to turn him over to the police! It's been bothering me all night. I think I'll run across as soon as I've had breakfast and see how's he's getting on."

"Oh, for heaven's sake!" said Dab-Dab wearily. "I know what that means. Now, you listen to me, John Dolittle; that boy could get along and take care of himself anywhere. Don't you worry about him."

"Yes, perhaps," said the Doctor. "But just the same—hulloa! What's this?"

At that moment two policemen in uniform appeared at the wagon door. Between them stood the red-headed boy.

"Heavens preserve us!" cried Dab-Dab. "Here he is, back again. And you were going to go after him!"

"Good morning, sir," said one of the policemen. "The Superintendent presents 'is compliments and says would you mind taking this young man back into your charge? Every effort, the Superintendent says, will be made to find his parents. But in the meantime if you wouldn't object to keepin' 'im, the Superintendent will be much obliged."

"Why," asked the Doctor, "wouldn't he stay with you?"

" 'E didn't seem to care for the station house, sir," said the constable. " 'Owled and 'ollered all night, saying 'e wanted to go back to the menagerie. And the Superintendent says— beggin' your pardon, sir—'e reckons that's the proper place for 'im. 'E's broke all the windows and nobody got a wink of sleep—prisoners and neighbours and every one complainin'. It seemed as though the only thing to pacify 'im was to fetch 'im back 'ere. So the Superintendent tells us to bring 'im and deliver 'im to you at all costs."

The small boy, now that he was back in his beloved circus, was wreathed in smiles. He greeted all the animals in turn—who didn't seem nearly as pleased to see him as he was to see them. The Doctor rose from the table a moment to put the canary cage out of his reach. And when he turned back to the door again he found that the two policemen had sneaked off without waiting for further words and left the young adventurer on his hands once more.

CHAPTER FOUR

THE GUEST DEPARTS

"Well," snorted Dab-Dab, "perhaps in the future you'll believe me, Doctor."

"Oh, yes, indeed, Dab-Dab. I agree that there's a lot in what you say," said John Dolittle as the young man pulled the lamp down on the floor with a crash. "Children are sometimes—er—a trial. But, you know, in some ways I'm sort of glad to see him back again—no, those geraniums don't need any more water, young man. I gave them some water before breakfast. Besides, that's hot water. You know, after all, Dab-Dab, this is a children's circus. It seems sort of proper that we should have one child on the staff."

"If you do you won't have anybody else on it—long," snapped the duck.

"Perhaps his parents don't mean to claim him at all," said the Doctor thoughtfully.

"Heaven forbid!" said Dab-Dab devoutly.

"Maybe we can train him," murmured the Doctor thoughtfully.

"No, those geraniums don't need any more water, young man"

"Then train him to keep away from me," said Dab-Dab, as the child upset the coffee-pot over the clean tablecloth.

Once more the Dolittle Circus was thrown into a state of turmoil by the return of the strange young person whose determination to be menagerie keeper had already caused so much trouble.

One of the first things to happen that day was the appearance of the circus' regular menagerie keeper at the door of the manager's van.

"I've come to give notice, Doctor," said he.

"Why, what's the matter?" asked John Dolittle.

"That young nipper's the matter," said the man. "I ain't 'ad no rest since 'e's been around. I warned you that I'd have to go unless he stayed away from my animals. Then when I 'eard 'e'd been took off to the police station I supposed we were going to 'ave some peace. But this morning 'e's back again and 'is interference and tricks is worse than ever. I want to give notice."

"Well," said the Doctor, "of course, if you've made up your mind. I wouldn't try to persuade you to stay. Have you got another position in view?"

"I don't need no other position," said the keeper. "Since you've been running the show on the sharing system I've saved up a tidy penny. And now we're in London I'd like to take a small shop somewhere and settle down."

"Oh, then it isn't only on account of the boy that you want to leave?" said the Doctor. "Well, I'm glad that you and your wife are able to take to the kind of life you prefer. After all, that's the most important thing. But I'll be sorry to lose you."

"There you are!" said Dab-Dab to Jip as soon as the man had left the wagon. "Another getting rich and retiring from the Dolittle Circus. While the Doctor goes on slaving without a penny to his name! Dear old Puddleby, will we ever see it again! I often wonder! All the Doctor ever saves up is new responsibilities and cares—like this young red-headed nuisance."

With the departure of the menagerie keeper the duties of

"You—you monster!"

Manager Dolittle and Matthew Mugg were increased. For until a new man was found to fill the post they had to take turns looking after the animals. And this was not made easier by the young adventurer, who insisted that he take the keeper's place and could hardly be kept out of the menagerie at any time.

But the next morning, to Dab-Dab's great delight, the youngster's mother at last turned up. When she demanded her child the Doctor took her over to the menagerie and, expecting her to be most delighted to find her boy safe, showed her the lad sleeping peacefully between the weary-eyed elephant's knees. With a shriek she clutched the child to her bosom and turned upon the poor Doctor in a fury.

"How dare you keep my son with your wild animals?" she screamed.

"But that was what he insisted on himself," said the Doctor. "I didn't want him to sleep here—neither did the elephant."

"I never heard of such heartless cruelty," yelled the woman. I'm going straight to the police station this minute. I'll have the law on you for this, you—you monster!"

In a storm of tears—in which the red-haired one joined—the woman departed—and did actually go and report the Doctor to the police. But, as it happened to be the same station which had harboured the young man for a night, the superintendent decided that the Doctor was more to be pitied than prosecuted and gave thanks that the young man was at last restored to the bosom of his family.

The End